A Bucket Full of Moonlight

And Other Stories

CHRISTOPHER J. BURKE

Pennsville, NJ

PUBLISHED BY
Paper Phoenix Press
A division of eSpec Books
PO Box 242
Pennsville, NJ 08070
www.especbooks.com

ISBN : 978-1-956463-65-1
ISBN (eBook): 978-1-956463-64-4

The titles contained in this collection were all previously posted to Reddit by the author.

All persons, places, and events in this book are fictitious and any resemblance to actual persons, places, or events is purely coincidental.

Cover Images obtained through www.shutterstock.com
Full moon. A huge moon reflected in the water.
   3D Illustration © Romanova Natali
Fantasy of neon waterfall in deep forest. Glowing colorful look like fairytale.
   2D Illustration. © Auxin

Cover Design: Mike and Danielle McPhail, McP Digital Graphics
Interior Design: Danielle McPhail, McP Digital Graphics

Dedication

To my first readers: Thomas, Rich, Rob, Laura & Jay, who gave me great feedback, suggestions, and encouragement, and who convinced me that there was more to some of these stories than I had originally written

Contents

I've Seen Empires Fall

"Empires rise and fall," the old man told me. He dropped his load onto a large stone and sat heavily beside it. He offered me a cup, and I filled it with cool water I'd hauled up from the well. He promised to pay me with a story as soon as he wet his parched throat. "I've seen a dozen pass into oblivion, far to the East, in the frigid North, and even closer to home."

Home? Did he mean here? "The last emperor to claim this land died 500 years ago. There's been nary a baron or crooked lord in that time that could depose the councils of elders who have held power ever since."

The traveler's mouth twisted in an attempt at a smile. A consumptive cough was the best laugh he could muster.

"Have you ever seen a city? Not a hamlet or town or village. A big city."

I snorted at the thought. I'm just a farmer. I've never been anywhere I couldn't walk to.

He continued, "I mean a big city, like the ones that border both sides of a river and stretch up into the hills or down to the seas? Those are powerful places. There's magic in the air and the soil, in the buildings and the people. And when that city is in the center of an empire, it's all that one thousand-fold. But few know how to tap into all that miraculous power. And the ones who can, they accumulate it for their own selves and not for the benefit of those over whom they rule."

I thought the old man mad, but entertaining. And I wished to hear more of this fantastical tale. So, I refilled his cup and asked a few questions. "If they were so powerful, why did they fall?"

He drank some more and sighed. "I'm sure you will agree with the ancient truth that power corrupts. The more who are corrupted, the more who will seek greater power of their own. Imagine that your well was drained faster than it could be replenished, and what remains is polluted. What would be the result?"

Sickness, I thought. *Disease. I would lose everything.*

When I looked at the traveler, he nodded as if he'd read my mind.

"Yes, the magic comes from the very souls of those cities, but inevitably, in the end, the magic dries up or becomes polluted. And when it does, the city does the same, infected from this pestilent pool. The buildings lose their gleam. The soil is tainted. The people flee. And the magic fades even faster."

I took some dried fruit from my pouch and offered it. The old man thanked me and ate it greedily.

When he was finished, I asked, "If the empire fell five centuries ago, how could you have seen the great cities?"

He stared at me with sunken eyes but his smile improved. "Magic lingers like embers of a flame. Longevity spells, cast at the height of my arrogance, while I sat on a throne of literal power, still faintly burn."

"*You* sat—?"

His face lit up as I made the connection, but like those embers, it too faded to ash. The ancient wanderer stood and thanked me again for the water. He put the cup back in his pack, which he then hoisted once more to his shoulder. Finally, he picked up his walking stick and leaned heavily against it.

"Yes," he said as he departed on his way. "I've seen many more than just five centuries. More than even five millennia. In those bygone ages, I have watched many empires rise and fall. And I fell with them."

As he walked down the road, I realized that he'd never told me his name. And yet I felt I already knew many of the names that he once went by. They were in the stories of my childhood that parents would tell around the fire. Cautionary tales of great and terrible times in faraway places. Now I knew that there was more truth in them than I'd ever believed. And yet, I felt an urge to go and see the magic myself.

For the first time in my life, I wanted to leave my farm and go see a big city.

Fallen Angels

Tantoque stood atop the slag pile and adjusted his fiery red tie. A gift from a successful haberdasher whose soul he'd one day claim, the tie matched the color of his sinful skin. He brushed down the deep black lapels of his suit jacket, and with the assistance of a little sulfuric spittle, he combed a clawed hand through the hair between his horns and batted down a wayward cowlick. He had to keep up appearances for the new arrivals.

A few moments later, however time was measured, he heard the first howls of terror and cries of anguish. Four demons, upright feral wolves with coats of fur like pointed steel wool, each drove a flock of horrified souls like slaughtered lambs to their torture. Each snapped an elongated whip of barbed wire to discourage stranglers. As the wretched columns crept along, each tormentor raised a fisted salute toward their master as they passed beneath his review.

Tantoque flashed the whitest, brightest smile that could be found in this region of Gehenna. He so enjoyed all the pomp and circumstance that accompanied the Orientation Day processions as the souls marched toward their eternal damnation. He loved the show, the spectacle, of it all. But unlike some of his peers, he let the duty of inflicting agony and anguish fall to devils of lower status. He was not like his rival Miseriae, who believed in conducting an explicit demonstration on a few of the unluckiest souls. Tantoque saw no need, nor held any desire to get his hands any dirtier than necessity required. And the feral wolves made all of it unnecessary. For now, at least.

As soon as the damned had disappeared from his sight and their gnashing of teeth had faded into the distance, he perambulated down the lee side of the slag heap toward the lava mansion he called home. Molded from molten rock, its shape was held by continuous obsidian flows. The basalt cobblestone walk was lined with rows of nightshade and henbane. Sulfuric fountains on each side proclaimed the great station of the house's owner.

And yet, like all things in Pandemonium, perhaps even more so, the facade belied what waited beyond the front door.

When Tantoque entered, he immediately dismissed his porcine skagservant and descended to his innermost sanctum. Once there, he'd be free of all prying eyes, except for the one nailed to the chamber door. Pity that the gorgol beast it formerly belonged to only had one eye to begin with. However, had it been a seven-eyed mesmer-demon, then seven stalks would adorn this portal. Either way, the warning had done its job for an eon.

He paused before the full-length mirrors lining either side of the hallway. Unlike the lesser demons that scurried about the house, he had no problem with seeing his own reflection. He rather enjoyed it, and always took Pride in his appearance. On his list of faults, Pride was number one with a bullet, which is why Tantoque felt the need to straighten his tie once more and to consider ripping the cowlick from his skull. But the flaws made the devil, after all, and it was better to own your flaw than allow it to own you.

With a satisfied smile, he took a deep cleansing breath and pushed open the door. Stepping across the threshold, he immediately spied the figure of a lovely fallen angel, in the literal sense of the word. Wings clipped; she lay on a tufted chaise longue. Her captor offered her comfort rather than the furnishings of a prison.

The angel lifted her head and addressed him. "How long will you keep me here, Tantoque?"

He noticed that the brilliance of her aura had dimmed a little during her captivity, yet beauty still radiated from her face cast by a light deep inside near impossible to extinguish. In fact, his presence in the room likely stoked the furnace within her, but sadly for the wrong reasons.

"Castitas, as always, you are free to leave. But a bird with broken wings cannot fly and would quickly fall victim to any passing predator." He took a seat on the opposite side of the room. "And there are many predators outside my doors."

The angel sat up and tried to spread her wings. Her face of determination faded into a wince of pain. Castitas wasn't you're everyday fallen angel. Her fall had not been of her choosing, but rather the result of wandering into a careless attack. She needed time to heal, and wings didn't grow overnight. Especially not in Hell.

"So I should settle for the devil I know? The predator inside the house? Even after all this time, I don't know your soul as anything other than something shriveled and twisted as a prune left too long in the sun."

He smiled. "And yet the prune was once a plum." Tantoque loosened his tie and slipped out of his jacket. "I admit that when I took you in, I was locking you away, but it is for your safety. Answer me truly, Castitas, have I ever shackled you to the wall? Tortured, beaten, or poisoned you? Have I ever, in any way…" He paused and nodded his head and raised his hands, palms out. "Forgive the word, have I ever attempted to molest you in any way?"

"'Forgive'? You would ask *me* to forgive *you* anything?"

He lowered his hands to his lap. "I assumed that was a hobby of your kind."

She turned her face away disgusted.

Tantoque stood and waved his jacket away. It rode a current of warm air and flitted into a closet. Then the devil sauntered to the liquor cabinet, pausing briefly to admire himself once again in the fiery cherrywood-framed cheval glass. Blasted cowlick! He retrieved a bottle and an absinthe glass, filling the latter with an unhealthy amount of anise.

"I confess that I am not perfect. I revel in the fact that I am not. And I would be more than happy to confront you on the field of battle were I not more of a lover than a fighter."

He turned back toward the angel. "Again, forgive me. Force of habit. You aren't my type. I prefer my mates more mean-spirited. Let us just say, I'd enjoy battling you for the soul of some living being. I'd happily stand on the sinister shoulder while you staked a claim on the dextral side. But I don't pull the wings from butterflies, nor torture the ones who've had them cut."

The devil's eyes narrowed as he restocked his bottle of spirits on the shelf. The corner of his mouth curled into a smirk. "Even now, how easy it would be to stick a pin through you and mount you on that wall, wings spread in all their splendor."

Tantoque lifted the glass, took a sniff, and drank deeply. "But where is the fun in that, hmm?"

The devil crossed the room to the fireplace. Once there, he eyed the infernal weapons mounted in the case above the mantel. Leaving them exposed was sort of a taunt as they would burn the angel's hand should she touch one. "That moment I found you, the thought of striking you down never entered my mind. Perhaps had it been one of my own denizens who had taken you down, I might have entertained the thought. A lucky shot on its part, to be sure. No doubt you learned a lesson in vigilance that won't soon be forgotten."

He removed a jewel-encrusted dagger from the rack. Rubies and sapphires sparkled with tiny bolts of flame while the obsidian blade sucked in all the light around it. Tantoque contemplated the utter blackness while balancing the dagger by its point on the tip of his middle finger.

"However, that wretched little gorgol beast, which you so readily dispatched even after it wounded you, scraped the bottom of a mighty chain of a command. The creature yanking that chain is the Vessel of Iniquity, Miseriae. You must have heard of him, no? One of the oldest of all devils from the time of the Fall. Where I am stern, he is vengeful. Where I am cunning, he is forceful. Where I may be cruel, he is filled with the wrath of ages."

The angel turned away from her unheavenly host. She believed herself to be just as safe presenting her back to him. And she didn't want to see his face. "I suppose I am to be grateful then? That you were the one who came upon me instead of him?"

"My dear." Tantoque let the dagger tip over. He caught the hilt in his palm and returned it to its proper place. "You are better off with me than if *anyone* of my kind had found you. But most especially Miseriae."

He returned to the bar and leaned against it. "Had a low creature of mine brought you down, I most certainly would have elevated its station—had you not so quickly dispatched it. In that case, my response to you would've been swift, possibly brutal, and most certainly clever.

"Miseriae, however, would have crushed that beast beneath his heel, ground it into the muck, so that it would remember its proper place in the natural order. And then you, my dear, would have experienced suffering unlike the worst you've ever witnessed or imagined. That endless noise I hear outside my home, that sound that fills these vast canyons and echoes off the crags, would be ten times louder. And that would all be from the ceaseless screams from your unending torment at his hands."

When Castitas whipped around to confront her devil, she thought she glimpsed him shudder before shaking it off. She watched him grab another glass and pour another drink.

"You sound like you both hate and admire him."

His laugh was cool, not maniacal. "You really don't know who he is, do you? Or should I say, who he was. Ah, but you were not formed yet when Lucifer fell. You didn't know the angels who were cast out in his company. Miseriae was among the highest of their numbers. Except that he wasn't expelled. He made a choice, of his own free will, to leave before he could be banished. As an angel, he was held in such high esteem that forgiveness could've been earned. There was a path to redemption were he truly penitent. You may have heard stories of his former life. He was known then as Misericordia. That is to say, Mercy. His name was *Mercy*!"

The devil paused to let the name sink in, but the angel sat frozen as an alabaster statue, unimpressed.

"Am I supposed to be shocked by the irony that your vile rival was named for one of the greatest Virtues?"

Tantoque shook his head from side to side and cackled. Some time passed before he could regain his composure. Castitas waited with a battle-tested patience she'd tempered throughout her captivity. He caught her steely gaze and laughed some more.

"Ages old but still a child," he poetically waxed into his tumbler. "My dear, Misericordia was not named after your esteemed virtue. It was the virtue that was named after him! He was the sire of mercy, if you will. And your Almighty saw this and said *It was Good*."

He hoisted his glass high as if toasting someone or something, then drank.

Castitas lost her temper, spitting, "This may be your home, but you will not mock Him in my presence!"

For the first time that afternoon, Tantoque showed his darker side. He placed his glass on the bar and took a step toward the couch. "I'll have you know that I loved Him — and lost Him — long before you were even a thought. It is out of respect that I do not allow His name spoken in this chamber. Respect, not fear. I have no fear of retribution. Down here, I am beneath the notice of His all-seeing eyes. He could see me if He chose. He chooses not to."

When his scowl faded, his cooler demeanor returned. "Now, where were we before this unpleasantness? Ah, yes. Your prison. I grant you that caging wild beasts is in my nature. However, I find that wounded creatures spark no joy, not with their majesty tarnished and their songs muted."

Filled with fury, the angel stood and marched toward the mirror. She turned her back to the cheval glass and peered over her shoulder. Her wings were healing, but very slowly.

"I'll spend half of eternity locked in this room at this rate. A never-ending nightmare."

The devil shrugged at the exaggeration. "And what would you have me do? No, really, tell me. I do have an interest in your eventual departure from this realm. What would speed their growth? I would wish to give you a swift recovery."

"I would wish to give you a swift kick to the ribs!"

"Feisty!" Tantoque bellowed out a laugh. "And I would likely deserve that kick. For now, however, I'm gladdened that you are in such good spirits despite everything."

Castitas pondered a moment. She shook her head and let out a sigh. "Not that I would want to accept any gift from you. What comes free would have too high a price attached. And what I would require, you could not supply."

He arched an eyebrow. "Try me."

"Would you consider sanctifying my prison?"

"My inner sanctum?"

"Yes." She returned to her seat and stretched out once more. "I knew that you would never consider it."

He put down the glass and retrieved the bottle for another pour. "No, I most certainly would not. However..." The devil swirled the liquid in the glass. "Suppose I could get you somewhere that is already sanctified?"

The angel bolted upright. Her face was hopeful yet guarded. "What corner of the Abyss would be sanctified instead of desecrated?"

"Who mentioned the Abyss? Or Hades? Or Hell? Or any of a thousand other perditious names? I make my own schedule, and while I delegate much of my responsibilities to subordinates so I can enjoy my leisure, I do take trips to the mortal realm. Not far from here is an obsidian bridge to that reality, one that leads to a cemetery across from a cathedral of... someone whose name I will not utter within these walls, though I might curse him on a slag heap. It is possible that I could get you as far as the first headstone. You'd have to make it on your own from there."

For the first time since her confinement began, a brief glimmer of celestial light sparked within her, enough to pierce the slithering shadows cast by the infernal flames which threatened to engulf her spirit and soul. In that instant, Hope swelled within Castitas. She spoke with an almost reverential tone to her most irreverential of hosts in this most inhospitable of places. "Whichever sai—, whichever *patron* the cathedral honors, I should do well enough until I can summon help from... from the Higher Planes." She looked her keeper in the eye, absent the hatred and malice that had been in her heart as long as she'd dwelt in this place. "If you can manage it."

He swapped out the tumbler for two fine crystal wine goblets and poured a dark red Malbec. He offered her one but the angel declined.

"It's a rather simple task gaining passage to the road we need to take. The trick is that smuggling you out will require quite a bit of deception."

Tantoque lifted the rejected wine glass and emptied its contents in a single gulp. He wiped his mouth with the back of his hand and smiled with a brightness that could rival the pearly gates.

"Luckily for you, my dear, I'm a master of tricks and deceit."

The angel's face fell, and she lowered her head. "Then my fate lies in treacherous hands."

"Nonsense! I will concede that point about treachery. However, as you have set a seemingly unattainable task before me, my pride will not allow me to fail. So you may be sure that I shan't let you down."

"But you *shall* hide me here until then. Do you have a scheme in mind to gain my freedom?"

Tantoque held up a single pointed finger. "Castitas, I believe the best way to free you may be, in fact, to hide you. Now, good subterfuge takes some time, but I have the perfect servant in mind who will prove most useful to you. I must bid you farewell, but I shall return soon."

As he turned to leave, his jacket flew out of the closet and landed on his outstretched arms.

Castitas held out an arm toward him. "Wait! I thought no one knew I was here."

"No one does," he replied, with a smile that would reassure the most cautious of souls. "Certainly, she does not. And regardless of what she learns, she will be in no position to act on that information for quite some time to come."

Horrified, the angel withdrew from her captor. "This may be a domain of torture, and those who dwell here are far from innocent. But

I would not wish any creature, condemned or hell-spawned, any added suffering because of me."

Tantoque fixed his tie, then slid his hands into his pockets and leaned back against the door. "And so, my dear, you *must* leave this place. Like the proverbial bat. Because just being here causes added suffering. Every day, there are creatures in anguish because of you. Because of your existence on this plane."

Castitas's face turned whiter than her robes. "Lies! How could I hurt anyone while locked in this room, O Treacherous Master of Deceit?"

He counted ten beats to level his temper, which only seemed to rile the angel more.

"I speak truly. Your presence here is an anomaly. Your aura radiates out through these walls. It projects a bubble, if you will, a bubble of mystic energy that has sparked a curiosity in those, near and far, who felt this perturbation in the air. There have been more than a few demons and devils that have sensed it, felt it get under their barbed, scaly skins. They've been drawn to it, have sought it out. And their curiosity, my dear, has led them to their ruination."

"You're saying that my aura has killed demons? From deep underground?"

"No, Castitas. I'm saying that I have killed them, under the charge of trespassing. That's why I keep you so far away on so large an estate. And yet you still attract them. I told you that I have an interest in seeing you depart this realm. That is it. I'm free to kill those who trespass against me, but some above me will eventually take notice of the sheer number of them suffering extreme abuse at my hand.

"So if you wish to prevent additional suffering, you must go. If you worry for my subordinate, fear not. She will earn a long vacation from this. I take care of those who serve me."

The angel's eyes narrowed to slits. "To be clear. You may be taking care of me, but I will never serve you."

Tantoque tried not to laugh. He failed. "My dear, I would never expect you to."

Time had lost much of its meaning in this unholy place. Castitas waited, looking for opportunities to flee, even knowing what dangers would lie beyond that door. Now it appeared that her road to salvation required a devil as her guide. He was the very definition of danger. And lies.

The angel's contemplation was broken by lock tumblers grinding for the first time in what seemed like ages. When the door swung wide, it revealed the ever-dapper Tantoque, well-groomed as always, except for those few stubborn hairs. He appeared to be dragging a lumpy, burlap sack behind him.

Was this seriously his plan, his great deceit? For the first time since her captivity began, Castitas laughed out loud.

Tantoque's eyebrows shot up at the sound. His face lit up to a brighter shade of red, and he couldn't help grinning along. He exclaimed, "The caged bird sings at last! May I ask what sparked your song?"

Had angels needed to breathe, Castitas might've collapsed at that moment being unable to do so. She pointed behind him, "Is that your master treachery? Stuffing me into a duffel bag and carrying me on your back? Or have you arranged for some hellish beast of burden to bear me?"

Puzzled for a moment, he realized what she referred to. "Ah, you misunderstand, and yet you are so close." He hauled the pile up and held it high in front of him. It was the hide, the empty shell, of a howler demon. "I have no plans to stuff you in or carry you. You can don it yourself and walk out of here on your own. With me as your escort, naturally."

"Naturally," the angel repeated, sardonically. Her arms were folded before her. "You honestly expect me to wear that?"

"Of course. It's a perfect disguise. We agreed that it would be best to hide you. Here is your hide. It may be a tight fit, but it will suffice in a pinch. And I fear that it will probably do more than just pinch."

"I can't possibly climb inside that! What were you thinking?"

"What were *you* thinking? That I'd crush some berries on your cheeks and try to pass you off as a succubus? Were I to burn your face with brimstone and peel your skin away, with you screaming exquisitely all the while, your inner light would burn all the brighter for it. This skin, however, will cover your entire form and should suppress your aura as we walk out of here."

"Should?"

"Despite the eons in which I've roamed these abysmal plains, this is entirely new territory for me."

"What happened to the creature that 'shed' that skin?"

"She's recovering in a lava pool. Call it a spa vacation. Just longer and quite a bit more painful. But before you know it, she'll be her old howling self again."

Castitas examined the pelt of coarse fur and rough leather that Tantoque pushed toward her. Reluctantly, the angel took hold of it. She yelped in pain and dropped it to the floor. Her hands were lightly singed. Even removed from the host, its husk still burned.

"Hmmm." The devil stroked his beard, contemplating this new wrinkle. "Perhaps I will have to help you dress after all. And we'll need to hurry once the hood is on and your face is covered."

"Your idea of helping me is to lock me inside a torture suit so I'll cry out in pain."

Tantoque steepled his fingers and tapped them against his chin. "Yes, that would help with the disguise. Do you think you can hit the same register? Howlers are a little higher and less melodic. Now, if you've finished with your objections, the sooner we start, the sooner your 'never-ending nightmare' will, in fact, end."

The angel collapsed into a chair, resigned to the purgatory she'd need to pass through. She tore the bottom of her robes and wrapped the scraps about her bare feet. Would that insolate her enough to allow her to walk? She knew she was about to find out.

She stared at the demon disguise on the floor. She didn't raise her eyes when she muttered, "Let's get this over with."

Tantoque stepped forward to assist. "Those are my five most favorite words."

Two figures walked down the basalt cobblestone path between the sulfuric fountains. The well-tailored devil strolled arm in arm with the matted-fur and leathery demon at his side. The odd coupling presented a sight to behold. But anyone who saw the pair leisurely perambulating across Gehenna would dismiss it as a lecherous assignation. Rank hath its privileges. None would question it. At least, none who feared the devil's wrath.

From the way she moaned and shuffled her feet, one might think her reluctant to participate. However, the way she kept her head lowered and leaned into her master might betray a hidden eagerness.

Tantoque felt the full weight of the hidden creature on his arm. He rather enjoyed the burden. The thought of an actual angel on his shoulder brought a smile to his lips. It might've been out of character for him to smile in public, but any observer would interpret it as either lustful or sadistic.

Every denizen of the realm gave the couple a wide berth. None dared to be accused of interrupting their leader while his attentions were occupied. And howler demons were terrifying in their own right, particularly ones that looked like they were writhing in heat.

As they negotiated a path between lava pools, Tantoque could feel a tinge of heat through the demon fur. He realized that Castitas was likely burning her way through the skin as much as it was burning her. Time was of the essence, and it seemed like that essence was rapidly fading. But the bridge was now in sight, guarded by only a pair of gorgol beasts. They scattered with a glare and a growl.

With the last impediment removed, the angel's escape was almost assured. Almost.

"What have we here?" boomed a deep, commanding voice behind them.

Tantoque spun about. There, larger than death, stood the great Iniquity himself, Miserae. He wore a magnificent uniform and cloak worthy of his station. He also wore a scowl that could level mountains.

"Parading around with something as low as a howler? Where are you going with her? She can barely walk."

Any show of weakness meant utter ruin. So the master of deceit simply smiled in reply. "After spending some time with me, they can barely stand. This one pleased me so that I fancied to treat her to some mortals before putting her back in her vault.

Miserae's eyes narrowed. He stepped forward, a massive arm outstretched before him. He was reaching for Castitas's hood. "Something feels off about this one. Don't you feel it? An aberration. There's an energy that's… wrong."

Tantoque froze in place. The senior devil locked eyes with his junior rival. "You *do* feel it! You are hiding something. Hand her over. Give her to me!"

Tantoque shrugged. "Okay. Have her. I've finished with her anyway." With that, he gave the costumed angel a shove. The floppy, saggy demon legs got tangled, and she fell into Miserae's arms.

When Miserae caught her, he felt a surge of excruciating grace course through him. "What is this?" he bellowed. The devil ripped back the hood to reveal the angel's marred face and vacant eyes. Even so, her beauty was not gravely diminished.

However, Castitas's strength had evaporated. Unable to hold her head up, her face fell onto Miserae's chest. It burned a hole through his garments and singed the flesh beneath.

He screamed louder than any banshee and pushed her to the ground. Then Miserae turned on Tantoque and growled. "This is severe treachery, even for you!" The once-favored Virtue, long ago corrupted, launched himself at his rival in a rage filled with hate of the ages.

Standing ready to receive the charge, Tantoque's mind mused that there had been a time when mercy could put an end to misery. And now the job had fallen to him to put an end to misery. It would be his cross to bear.

The two collapsed in a heap on the ground. But a moment before their collision, Tantoque withdrew an unsheathed obsidian dagger from his sleeve. The blade drank in all the light of the fires between them. He leveled it and punched it through the singed skin in the center of Miserae's chest until only the ruby- and sapphire-encrusted handle remained. The blade absorbed the devil's essence until it drained its vessel dry.

Tantoque pushed his attacker off him and retrieved his dagger. There would be hell to pay sometime down the line. Miserae's spirit would eventually return from whatever condemnation his soul had fallen to. For now, his empty husk could rot in the muck. There were more pressing concerns.

The surviving devil stood. He started to brush the clay from his suit then stopped himself. His vanity would have to wait. Wandering demons and random beasts might summon foolish bravery against a perceived weakness. And mystical, angelic energy pouring forth from his caged bird could summon any number of those beasts.

Covering her face once more, Tantoque lifted the prone angel into his arms. He screamed once at the sudden burst of righteous heat he felt. Then, step by step, he climbed the ramp to the obsidian bridge leading to the mortal realm. He had a task to complete. *No,* he thought, *it is more of a promise.* Devils may twist their words, but in the end, they also kept them.

Their progress through the planes was marked by the deepest black volcanic stone fading to a dull gray slate. When they reached the end, they emerged beneath a thousand pinpoints of light twinkling in a moonless sky.

Tantoque stumbled to the asphalt. The bundle in his arms rolled free into the grass, coming to rest against the first obelisk. The monument was inscribed with family names extending back over a century. It held the power of several generations of souls. The devil was powerless to continue forward, could not assist in any way. Despite his promise to free her, the devil couldn't release the angel from the straitjacket he'd imprisoned her inside.

Slowly, he stood and crept to the grass's edge. He spun about, surveying the area. Was there anyone or anything that could aid him? That's when he heard a scream behind him. The eruption of energy he felt at his back drove him down to his knees.

Tantoque shifted his body around on the pavement. He saw the demon suit had burst into flames, blazing bright orange and red, and spitting out tongues of fire. He heard Castitas crying out from within. Slowly, the pitch of her voice changed as the infernal conflagration shifted, first to blue and then white until it was reduced to little more than a shapeless ball of pure light without form hovering above the hallowed ground. The devil couldn't move forward, but neither could he move away. He just knelt there, rooted in place, mesmerized.

Sparks burst across the night air like swarms of confused fireflies. Several settled on Tantoque's suit and burned pinholes between the pinstripes. Searing flecks hit his face and hands, blistered his scarlet skin. The devil felt an intensity of heat he'd never before encountered. Never in the bowels of the Earth nor on any plane of any underworld. Something forged in the hottest furnaces can still buckle and melt when faced with greater, harsher temperatures. And yet, despite this inferno, he made no effort to rise and flee.

"Fascinating," he muttered to himself. When you gaze into the bliss, the bliss gazes into you. "Beautiful."

That ball of light blazed brighter than any star. It sparked a memory of the burning flame at the heart of Creation. As he stared into it, Tantoque thought he saw a shape emerging. Inside the brilliant sphere, he spied a figure being molded like clay. *Castitas?* The image formed into a naked silhouette standing before a blinding spotlight.

Radiant beams drew closer to him, scorching his beard, cracking his skin. Searing his heart. Tantoque watched what he could only imagine as an angelic rebirth. Enraptured, he gave no thought to his own imminent destruction. He only hoped that he would get to see her. If one such as he was worthy of a final wish, that is what it would be. One last glimpse was all he desired ere he perished forever in unquenchable fire.

Then a heavenly voice sang out, "For one such as you, there can be no Redemption. But there can be Mercy."

A shapely leg emerged from the brilliance. Swiftly, it kicked forward. The foot caught Tantoque squarely in the chest.

The devil was propelled backward, off the Earthly plane. He landed somewhere along the obsidian bridge. The otherworldly flames had been extinguished from his skin, hair, and clothing.

Tantoque sat up and rubbed his chin and the remains of his beard. All he wanted to do was to return to his empty inner sanctum and pour a stiff drink. Several drinks, in fact. Then he looked down at the distinctly feminine footprint emblazoned on his ribcage. He realized that he'd carry that mark for a long time. It would be best to keep it hidden. Suddenly, that thought of the necessity of hiding this heavenly reminder bore his spirits aloft. He laughed out loud. "I probably deserve that."

Headhunter for the Angels

"Judy, send in my 3 o'clock."

The expected reply came through the intercom speaker on the desk. *"Yes, Mr. Birnbaum."* It was followed by an unexpected, *"Mr. Birnbaum! There's a prob —"*

He stared at the intercom, waiting for Judy's voice to complete that sentence. Birnbaum was about to press his finger on the button, when he saw strange lights flickering and flashing through the frosted glass pane in the door separating his office from the reception area and Judy's desk. He sat back mesmerized, unable to move. Then the door opened, and the room was filled with radiant beams, which bathed the man behind the desk in their warmth.

Through the brilliance, Birnbaum saw three silhouettes walk in. *Are those Men?* he wondered. *Women? Beings of some kind?* They each had strong, stern faces, and wore long, white, lustrous gowns. Birnbaum had to squint just to look at them. He couldn't tell if the garments were robes or togas or even electric overcoats stolen from a wardrobe department down Shubert Alley.

Whatever they were, they were brighter than any bulb from any marquee.

His voice died in his throat for a moment, but he managed to call out. "You're not my 3 o'clock!"

"No." A voice filled his ears, but he couldn't tell who had spoken. "No, George Birnbaum. I'm afraid that your '3 o'clock' will have to wait. We have more pressing concerns."

Birnbaum raised a hand up to his shield his eyes. He had to turn his head away. "Okay. More pressing concerns. I hear you. But could you tone that down a little so I can also see you?"

Almost immediately, the brightness of the room returned to ambient level.

"Is that better?"

"Yes, thank you." As his eyes adjusted, Birnbaum could see that his visitors all appeared to be men costumed in what he assumed to be some kind of religious garb. "Now, er, gentlemen? What brings you into my office?"

The three heavenly beings floated across the floor as they approached the man's desk. "Do you know who we are?"

"I have an inkling of what you're supposed to be. Are you part of a magic act? A circus troupe? I don't usually work the entertainment field, but I have a few connections. Now if you can make an appointment with Judy outside, we can schedule a meeting."

He reached for his phone. The nearest of the angelic trio waved a hand, and Birnbaum's hand froze in place. A second pointed, and the phone disappeared.

"Okay," said the frightened executive. "You have my attention."

"I am Michael. This is Gabriel and Raphael. We have come down from Heaven, and we are in need."

"Riiiight." Birnbaum nodded. "And what can I do for you... 'Angels'?"

Raphael spoke up. "We have an opening that we need filled."

"Immediately," Gabriel added.

The headhunter grabbed a legal pad with his left hand. He tried to move his right hand and realized it was still frozen. He gave it a tug, and it was free again, allowing him to pick up a pencil.

"Fine. What's the position?"

The three spoke in unison. "God."

"God?"

Michael nodded. "Yes, God. He appears to be... away for the moment, and we need a temporary replacement."

"Away, you say. For the moment." Birnbaum was about to complain that his was not a temp agency but thought better of it. Oftentimes, short-term contract work led to many lucrative opportunities later on. "Okay, so describe the type of person you're looking for. I suppose you'll need someone strong, someone powerful..."

"That is incorrect," said Gabriel. "Power and strength will flow to him—or her—from the Faithful. We are not expecting omnipotence and omnipresence. These qualities will not be found on this plane."

The pencil tapped the pad as the man thought. "Okay. So, what is it that you do need?"

"Someone good," replied Michael. "Good and loving. Wise, if possible, but we can provide counsel. The candidate will have the heavenly hosts at his beck and call to assist with all job responsibilities."

He scribbled notes on the pad. "I can make a few calls. How long is the position for?"

The three shared a moment, glancing back and forth. Michael spoke for the trio, "At this time, we are uncertain."

"Ah, so there's a possibility that they can be picked up for a long-term commitment. That may open up the field of candidates quite a bit. I assume that would include the usual benefits, correct? Health? Pension? Excellent. I just need some information. How can I contact you?"

Gabriel stepped forward. "Here, take my horn."

Take his horn? Birnbaum thought. *Are these jokers serious?*

Birnbaum stood and leaned across his desk, hoping that playing along would get them out of his office sooner. However, he misjudged the size and weight of the four-foot instrument and nearly stumbled as soon as Gabriel released it.

"Excuse me. It's a little heavier than it looks."

Gabriel met the man's eyes and stared beyond them. "The horn is only as heavy as one's soul, George Birnbaum. Is there something troubling your soul?"

"What? No. Of course not." As soon as the denial left his mouth, the weight of the horn seemed to shift in his hands. He resisted the temptation to drop it onto his desk.

Michael stepped forward. "We shall take our leave, George Birnbaum. We will await your call." His wings spread as he bowed his head. Then he stepped back.

Birnbaum nodded back with a smile on his face and a tight grip on the horn. Whatever this meeting was, it was almost over.

"I'll be happy to make some cal—"

A sudden flash blinded him. Dazzling white light danced in his eyes like a swirling blizzard. When he could finally see again, Birnbaum found himself sitting, gripping the arms of his leather chair. The horn stood upright on his desk next to the phone, which had reappeared. He felt liked he'd gotten up too quickly when he hadn't stood at all. His head was light. His heart was heavy. And his soul…

Was his soul troubled?

Staring, eyes fixed, into the void between the desk and the door, George Birnbaum felt his anxiety yield to the serene calm that washed over him. He didn't move until Judy buzzed that she was leaving for the day.

Curious, he thought. *She didn't mention the men she'd seen enter the office. Or the fact that she never saw them leave.*

When Birnbaum returned to his office the following day, the horn stood on his desk like a beacon. If he'd only imagined the incident the day before then his part of the hallucination was quite persistent. He made a wide circle around his desk before sitting down with his morning coffee and bagel.

He felt an urge to dispose of the matter, and the horn, but was unsure how to go about it. He had contacts in finance, retail, and pharmaceuticals. He'd place many project managers and department heads. Could he find someone to fill an unfillable position.

And would anyone take his phone call seriously?

Taking a sip of his coffee, he decided he'd wait a while before reaching out. He'd see what the next couple days of interviews might bring.

Unfortunately, the pool of mostly IT specialists and middle management didn't yield any candidates. While the horn made for an interesting conversation piece, none who were curious enough to try lifting it were actually able to do so.

"It's deceptively heavy," George said, adding a forced laugh.

The problem, as Birnbaum saw it, was that the people on the other end of the resumes tended to be too obnoxious, too ambitious, arrogant, or proof of the Peter principle.

And not Saint Peter, either.

He couldn't present the angels — and he'd begun to believe that they were, in fact, angels — with a borderline narcissist to fill the sandals one of who created mankind in his own image. Birnbaum didn't want to imagine how that could play out.

After three days of staring at the musical obelisk before him, Birnbaum was ready to admit defeat. He'd found his way out of hopeless causes before, but this challenge was too much.

He was contemplating blowing the horn to admit his failure when Judy entered the office with a folder of papers.

"These need your signature, Mr. Birn—"

She stopped when she saw Gabriel's horn.

"Oh. When did you bring that in, Mr. Birnbaum? I didn't even know you played an instrument."

He leaned back in his chair and shook his head. "I... don't, actually."

Judy tilted her head to consider that for a moment and then went to place the open folder flat on the desk. She picked up the horn to make room.

"Is it okay if I put this on the table over here, Mr. Birnbaum?"

Birnbaum's hand froze in the middle of a dismissive wave. He looked up from his desk and stared into Judy's eyes. She leaned back a little.

"Judy, do you play?"

Raising a hand to her heart, she said, "Me? No, not at all. Not even a tin whistle."

He stood and stepped toward his secretary. Waving at the horn, he encouraged her, "Try the horn. Give it a toot."

Judy blushed. "No, I couldn't..."

"Nonsense. Just one little puff and see what happens. I mean, maybe you're a natural."

It was the weirdest thing her boss had ever asked of her, but it seemed tame enough. She shrugged her shoulders, smiled, and brought the horn to her lips with ease. When she blew into the mouthpiece, the other end heralded the arrival of someone important.

And in a flash, three important figures appeared in the office.

When her eyes had cleared, Judy was frozen in awe of the heavenly trio standing before her.

"We heard your summoning, George Birnbaum. And we have returned."

"Judy." Birnbaum placed a hand gently on her shoulders and turned the other in the direction of the newcomers. "May I present to you Michael, Raphael, and Gabriel. You may have read about them in your studies."

The woman's chin quivered. "They're the... They're the... I remember now... Mr. Birnbaum. You know... you actually know... *angels?*"

"They're recent acquaintances." The man thought better than to lie or exaggerate in their presence. His heart light, he attempted to retrieve Gabriel's horn, but he had difficulty freeing it from Judy's grasp.

Gabriel floated over to Judy and placed his hand around hers, and her grip loosened.

Judy started to kneel but the angel shook his head and kept her upright.

"George Birnbaum." Michael stepped forward. "We see that you have found a suitable applicant. Hello, Judy."

Movement returned to Judy's extremities, and her head started to clear. "Applicant? For what? I didn't apply for anything."

Raphael gave a side glance to Birnbaum, who unable to meet his gaze, looked to the floor.

"Nevertheless, Judy Schaefer, you have the right qualities we need for the position."

Judy shook her head. "What are you talking about? What position."

"God," Birnbaum said.

"God?"

"God," the angelic trio confirmed in unison.

"But I can't be God! That's… that's… not right. I mean, I aspire to be like Him. I've never aspired to actually be Him."

Michael touched a finger to Judy's forehead, and her quivering ceased. "Surely, one who desired to be Him could never be. Your reluctance comes from Grace. But we are in need of your assistance. Will you help us?"

Once more, Judy was speechless.

Birnbaum prodded her, asking "Are you going to turn down the request of three angels?"

Judy blinked three times and swallowed once. "Well, no. I couldn't do that. Yes, I'll help you."

"Thank you, Judy Schaefer," Michael said.

The three angels knelt before her and bowed their heads. Before Judy could speak, there was one final flash of light.

When Birnbaum's eyes cleared, he was alone in the room. Judy, the angels, and that blasted horn had all vanished. He sat down at his desk and saw the papers awaiting his signature.

"One position filled, and another opens up," he mused.

Then he sighed when he realized that he'd need to make a bunch of phone calls. Finding a temp for God was one thing. Finding another secretary like Judy, now that was going to be the real challenge.

Blood Totem and Eggs, Wreck'Em

VULGORE THE TORMENTOR SAT AT HIS USUAL BOOTH WITH THE TABLE pushed away just enough to accommodate his swollen abdomen. He was sipping flaming-hot coffee when a shadow fell across his menu. Looking up from the breakfast specials, he saw Mighty Giramando the Transpiercer, except that he appeared less mighty and fierce and more haggard and disheveled.

"Geez, Jerry," the Tormentor said. "You look like all the Hells! You been trollin' through the deep planes of the Abyss again?"

Giramando's robust shoulders drooped. His immense chest sagged into his belly like that of a middle-aged man moments after a nubile lass passed from view. He slumped heavily into the booth, which was braced to support devilish creatures of his mass.

As soon as he sat, a cup and saucer appeared before him as if apparated. Deomica, Waitress of the Dark, stood over him with a fresh pot of Lava Java. Her Sin Café smock barely contained her topless human half and hung down to an inch above her hairy goat knees. She poured out a cup and gave the Transpiercer a wink. "The usual, Jerry?"

He returned a pained, twisted smile and nodded with a grunt. Deomica scribbled on her pad and turned away.

"Hey," Vulgore called out. "What about me? Can I get *my* usual, too?"

"Whatever." Deomica paused to add the extra order to the ticket. She shook her rump at the disfavored demon, almost daring him to smack it. But Vulgore knew he'd lose his paw if he tried. So he just sat quietly and watched as she cantered away toward the grill. A moment later, he heard her call out, "Adam and Eve on a raft, toss 'em out of Paradise!"

A guttural voice from the kitchen hollered back. "You know I hate that! Get it right!"

The two demons in the booth ignored the staff fight and returned to their coffee.

"I didn't get any sleep last. Again!" Giramando complained. He took another sip and felt the sweet, sweet burn. "Three times I was summoned. Ever since that goth kid found my blood totem in that pawn shop last month, they haven't left me alone!"

Vulgore put his cup down. "Geez, Jer, that's rough. Why so much? Do goth kids have that many enemies they needed hunted down?"

Giramando sighed. "At least impaling and disemboweling their adversaries might be worth some of the effable expense. But every single one of them wants the same thing!"

The Tormentor did a five-count by drumming his fingers on the table. He snorted twice in the awkward silence and then gave in. "Which is?"

"They all want to be different. *Just like everybody else!* And so, this kid Jason realized that he could be the most different by having a demon friend to 'hang with.' His coven compadres were all in awe of his consorting with his 'Main DF.' Next thing you know, each of them is taking a turn calling me, tugging on that choking totem leash!"

"Taking turns? Without smiting any of their rivals? Why? What purpose does 'hanging with' serve?"

"It increases their 'cred'."

"Their crud?"

"Their cred! Don't ask me. I haven't picked up the lingo yet."

Scratching behind his anterior cranial horns, Vulgore considered the situation. "If this Jason wanted to be different, why did he pass around your totem?"

The tormented Giramando drained the remainder of his mug. The burning sensation fired up his gizzards something fierce. He felt some strength returning. "He didn't. This other kid, Phillip, stole it."

Vulgore laughed. "Well, you have to admire that, Jerry."

"After a fashion," Giramando grunted and nodded his agreement. "Then it was stolen from Phillip by Rory, who gave it Lauren for impure reasons of his own. Can't blame the kid for trying. After that, Lauren shared it with a half dozen more before Jason seized it again."

"Seized? Gotta respect that, too. I mean, it sucks for you, but jealously guarding possessions is something you can work with. Speaking of possessions…"

The deflated demon shook his oversized noggin. "They haven't dropped their guard enough yet to let me slip in. Not while they have the blood in that totem. This one kid, Chas, found mystical manuals in some web-covered space that gave away too many secrets. The 'wicked keys,' he called them. Or the 'wikis.' That Chas is the worst of the bunch."

Vulgore held up the six fingers of his sinister hand. "You said a half dozen." Then he ticked off four more on his right for Jason, Phillip, Rory, and Lauren. "That's ten all together. Do you think you could get them all together at one time with two more?"

The mouth of the other demon widened to the point where it almost split his face in two. "I've been waiting for it. Word is getting around. It shouldn't be much longer before a couple more loner punks want to join the band. Then we can have my kind of party."

Giramando started shuffling the condiment jars around the table. "When I have twelve of them in one circle with myself in the center?" He scooped up the bottle of habanero sauce and held it tightly in his fist. Then he waved it over the other condiments. "I'll sprinkle my blood totem over the lot of them. Then I'll perform a little ritual of my own. One that lets me devour one or two of those kids and make bound disciples out of the survivors. Then I'll be the one holding the leashes.

"It's what I hold out hope for, as much as a demon can hope."

The two chortled and guffawed thinking of the feast to come. Vulgore raised a hand over the table for a High Six, and Giramando slapped it.

"Playing the long game, I love it! Make sure you post a note to my pit, Jerry. I won't wait on you for breakfast that morning!"

The Transpiercer reached inside a fold in his scaly skin. "In the meantime, I have this." He pulled out a jar that was half-filled with tiny points of colored lights. They flitted about like fireflies. He set in on the table between the two of them.

"Hot, hopping Hells, Jer! That's some Soul Jar! I can't remember the last time I saw one so full."

"The thought of filling it and earning a vacay to Tahiti has kept me going."

"How'd you manage it?"

He put both great paws flat on the table. "Chas may have found a manual, but he obviously didn't understand the whole thing. There's a repeater clause. When the owner of the totem calls upon me again, I'm able to slice off tiny pieces of their souls. Chas seems to believe that with each new owner, the slate is clean. So they avoid summoning me twice in a row before passing the totem on to the next one. But—"

"But—" Vulgore worked it through in his head. "But Lauren gifted the totem to everyone in their coven. They all have possession every single time."

Giramando sat back and hefted his massive chest. He pushed his cup to the edge to await a refill when he noticed Deomica trotting their way with two platters and another pot of java.

"Orders up, sweetie." She gingerly set a plate of scrambled eggs and toast in front of him. Then tossed the other one down to Vulgore, splattering his eggs in purgatory and knocking the toads out of their holes.

"Hey! Watch it, Deo!"

"Bite me!" she snarled. Her sweet façade snapped back into place when she turned back to the Mighty Transpiercer. Her voice became softer and sultry, and she playfully snapped her teeth together.

"You can bite me, too."

The copper-skinned satyress gave him another wink and refilled their cups, spilling only a few fiery drops on Vulgore to torment the Tormentor.

"Thanks, doll," Giramando said. He picked up the Soul Jar and carefully reached into it. He managed to pinch a tiny blue dot of light between a massive finger and thumb. Pulling it out, he made an offering of it to Deomica. "Here's a little Chas for you. He's been busting my rump, maybe he'd like to try yours."

"In his dreams!" She held the point of light in the center of her palm, which took on a deep violet tinge like an ugly, violent bruise.

"His dreams would be a good place to start," Giramando replied, adding his best fiendish smile. "That piece should get you into them. I'm sure you'll take it from there in ways that only you could."

A lascivious smirk crossed her lips. "You always know the way to a gal's heart, 'Piercer. I can't wait for the end of my shift." Then after tucking her tip into her smock, she trotted away. This time, Giramando enjoyed the view.

"She's sweet on you, Jerry. Like mango salsa. Or a chipotle margarita."

Vulgore seized the habanero and scattered it across his breakfast. He stabbed a hunk of meat from his plate, and shook it in his friend's direction. "You're stealing the souls of greedy teens and the heart of a lusty waitress. You know something? You're incorrigible, Jerry."

Giramando stuffed a massive pile of eggs into his mouth but spoke through it. "I try."

"If it gets to be too much for you, throw a little of the action my way? 'Kay? The souls, I mean. Not Deo. Unless she's got a friend. Or an enemy. Even a frenemy."

Having finished his breakfast, Giramando sat back and patted his fully, bloated belly. A satisfying belch escaped. Last night had been miserable, but his day was starting to brighten up. The long game was about to pay off.

Have I Got a Deal for You

FRANKIE SAW THE MAN EYEING THE CANDY-APPLE RED CONVERTIBLE. HE wore a nicely pressed suit and exuberated confidence. With a few character lines on his face and touch of gray at the sides, there was a richness to his complexion that could only be rivaled by his wallet. This was a refined gentleman of taste who knew what he wanted. And it was Frankie's job, and his pleasure, to give it him, for a reasonable price, plus commission.

And thus began the timeless refrain to the dance between salesman and customer.

With hand outstretched, Frankie approached his new client. "You've picked out a beauty, Mr. — ?"

"Skag," he replied. Like a wax figure from Madame Tussaud's, he stood immobile and yet full of life. He chose not to remove either hand from his pockets as he addressed the dealer. "Call me, Skag."

Smiling, the agent drew back his arm without looking away from the gentlemen's reddened eyes. "Well, Mr. Skag, it's nice to meet you. I'm Frankie Kilkenny, and I can see you are a discriminating person."

"Indeed," he replied, with a matching smile of his own. "Very much so."

"You've reached that place in life where you want to pamper yourself in luxury. I've seen it before. Other distinguished men of means, some older than you..."

"Oh, I hardly think so."

"...who wanted to ride in style. But, unlike you, those were not decisive men. They didn't chase their dreams. They hesitated and were lost. But I can tell that that is not who you are, sir. Am I right? You're someone who goes after want he wants?"

Skag's grin nearly cleaved his face into two. "Oh, yes. Most certainly, I do. And that's why I came in here today. There is most certainly something here that I want."

Could it get any easier than this? Frankie mused. Curiously, reading Skag's face, he wondered if the gentleman was thinking the same thing.

"And that is why I want to make you a deal today. I want to see you drive this baby off the lot before these doors close this evening! If you would step this way toward my office."

Frankie pointed an arm in one direction while swinging the other behind Mr. Skag to usher him along. The office turned out to be little more than a glorified cubicle that sat at the end of the row of dealers' desks. Frankie's was a smidge larger and had a touch more privacy, but it was, nonetheless, still a cubicle.

"Actually, Mr. Kilkenny, I'm here to make *you* a deal."

Frankie stopped in his tracks. He looked his prospective client in the eye, noting that it had deepened to a darker shade of red. The longer he looked, the more it had almost a faint glow about it. Then he noticed that just below the man's hairline, two small bumps protruded from Skag's forehead. They had the look of the stumps where vestigial horns once grew... except that in that moment those two stumps grew out an extra quarter inch.

"You see, Mr. Kilkenny —"

"Frankie! Please, call me Frankie!" Retaining his salesman's smile, he displayed no outward sign of distress and kept his cool in the face of what was happening.

"Ah, but Kilkenny is such a lovely name. However, if you insist, Frankie, I've come with an offer that you can't refuse."

Frankie offered Skag a cushioned seat and sat himself in the padded leather chair on the other side of the desk. "Well, that is more than kind of you, Mr. Skag. You know, I loved that movie. Oh, man, that *horse!* Am I right? And speaking of horses, that little baby you were admiring has the power of 500 horses under its hood, along with a five-liter V8 engine. She's ready to go from zero to *Bat of out Hell* in no time."

Skag offered a polite laugh. "I see that we have a bit of an understanding here. You are a very clever man, Mr. Kilken... Frankie. You can really go places."

Frankie, not being someone who ever lost his sense of humor before a client, chuckled in response. "And I do go places! Florida, the Mediterranean, I love going places that are sunny and warm. Though I have to say, I'm not too keen on dark, dank, or boiling hot. But were I to go somewhere like that, I'd want to cruise straight through with the wind in my hair, riding on 20" forged aluminum wheels, and with my GPS pointing the way."

The demon's horns burst through its skin, and his veins bulged along his neck. "Oh, nowhere like that, my friend. Perish the thought! I was thinking about going to your own dealership or your own chain of dealerships. Picture yourself managing your own employees, with dozens of beautiful young ladies modeling the cars for so many appreciative customers. You seem the type to like the young ladies, am I right? Or young gentlemen, if you prefer. I'm not *that* discriminating."

Frankie held up his left hand and wiggled his fingers for a moment to highlight his wedding band. "If you wish to talk about ladies, let me say that that beauty on the floor is a magnet for them! And it will fit four of them comfortably. Now, just between us, you seem like someone can handle the kind of trouble that four young ladies can provide. And I bet you like 'em young."

The demon started to speak, but Frankie cut him off. "I know — to you, they're *all* young. But what *isn't* young is the deal I can give you on that little lady. There are offers that are expiring even as we speak, with rebates for limited times. And you look like a gentleman, or a thing that looks like a gentleman, who prepares in advance for those end times. Am I right, Mr. Skag?"

Skag eyed his prospective client, contemplating how to sweeten his pot. "What about you, Frankie? Are you prepared for the end times? How would you like to leave this world? Sitting at a desk? Or lounging by the pool at your mansion? One of your many mansions."

Both salesmen considered each other.

"Would the mansion have a multi-car garage?"

Skag's forked tongue flicked out to lick his upturned lips, before slithering back between a pair of canine fangs. "Of course, what would a mansion be without a huge garage, loaded with the finest examples of automotive splendor? It would have the best cars from all your showrooms from around the globe, all at your disposal."

The car dealer leaned forward, elbows on his desk planner, "And you're sure you're picking out the best of the best? The finest in the world?"

The dream dealer leaned in to close the gap. "Of course. I would only want the best."

"In that case..."

"Yes...?"

Frankie sat back in his chair. A contract had appeared in his hand, as if by magic, and he slapped it down on the desk. "In that case, you'd want that beauty over there! You want its 8-speed automatic transmission with overdrive, 4-wheel anti-lock brakes, integrated navigation system, side-seat-mounted airbags, driver and passenger knee airbag and airbag occupancy sensors!"

The demon shifted in his chair. "What?"

"Did I mention the satellite radio and USB ports? Plus, it has front *and rear* cupholders!"

"What? No. What?" A pen suddenly appeared in the demon's hand.

"And Skag! *Beelzebubbala*! If you sign right now, I can knock a point off our 2.9% financing, and I'll throw in a coupon for a reduced-price paint job in case you want more of a lava red exterior."

"But — but — wouldn't you like — ?"

"What I'd like is to see you, Skag, driving down the main drag through Hell's Kitchen with four of the hottest succubi just melting into those plush seats. Don't worry, they're coated with our special stain-resistant treatment, at no extra cost. Or are you a hellhound kind of helldude? A man and his dog: a classic, for all the ages! And you've seen all the ages, am I right?"

The two locked eyes and exchanged trustworthy smiles.

Skag faltered first.

"Trust me!" Frankie circled in for the close. "These payments are so reasonable you won't have to sell your soul." He moved in closer and whispered with a wink. "Unless you want to."

My Own Personal Hell

WITH A TWIST OF THE TAP, THE HOT WATER SPLASHED INTO THE BASIN. Steam rose and fogged the mirror. I was in a fog of my own as I watched as my reflection slowly fade away, vanishing from sight. When I'd completely lost myself, I wiped a hand across the damp surface and brought it all back. Reset. Repeat.

In between the cycles, I lathered up and removed the stubble, mindful of yesterday's nicks, but not quite mindful enough.

A few new ones appeared. I went to dispose of the razor but stayed my hand. It was the last in the pack, and I might not get a chance to pick up another. Maybe I could get one more shave out of it. I just had to be more careful.

When I dragged myself back to the master bedroom, I saw that Rosa had walked in. She was waiting less than patiently and had that stern expression on her face. Rosa looked at me and then glanced at my black suit on the bed. I stood there, somewhat embarrassed, clad solely in an undershirt and boxers.

"You're not dressed yet. Why aren't you dressed? We have to go soon. The limo is on the way. I swear you'd be late for your own funeral."

That last word twisted a knot in my stomach. "I get the feeling that I was," I said. I picked up my white dress shirt and removed it from the hanger. "In a past life, maybe."

Rosa skirted the bed and yanked the shirt from my hand. She started to stuff me in it, reducing me to a child whom she had to dress for Church. I stood still, not daring to move.

"If you can't hold it together for your mother," she scolded, "how will the kids be able handle losing their grandmother."

"Again, you mean?"

"What are you talking about? My mother's alive."

My mind still clouded, I had to stop to think. What was it that I was talking about? "I mean the service we had for my mother last month."

Rosa sighed. "Are you talking about the memorial service we had after the accident? Your whole family needed that then." She looked around for my tie. When she'd scooped it up, her fiery eyes looked like she was about to squeeze a size 15 knot around my size 17 neck. "We decided to wait for your Uncle Tim and Aunt Marjorie to come back from Europe to have the Mass and burial at the cemetery."

"Right. Tim and Marjorie." I tried to picture the two of them in my mind but couldn't see them clearly. I dropped my eyes to the floor and watched my toes bunching clumps of the carpet. "They're not coming back either, are they."

Rosa held my face in her hands, her tenderness mixed with a little impatience. "No dear. Such a tragic thing for their ship to sink."

That would be the next funeral. I wondered if my suit could survive another one so soon.

Cuff links appeared in my hand. "Can you manage those on your own? I have to see if Jess and Robbie are ready to go."

Jess and Robbie, I repeated in my mind. *Jess and Robbie. Jess and Robbie... and Eileen.* How long had Eileen been gone now? Was she still with us at mom's last birthday party? That was the small one we had two weeks after Uncle Benji had passed. Which happened not long after Dad died. Which happened after...

"Do you ever think about Eileen?" I called out.

Rosa stopped in her tracks a foot from the door. She turned, filled with a fusion of sadness and anger. "How dare you."

It wasn't a question.

"I know you're grieving but that doesn't mean that I'm not. Of course, I think about my baby. All the time."

I held up a hand. "It's just, when I think of her, when I remember her, I only see her crying. Crying at my father's funeral. Crying at her cousin Michelle's wake. Crying... crying at Robbie's hospital bed... when he died... after the car accident that killed my mother."

Those words hung in the air. The accident that killed my mother happened over a year ago. And it happened last month. Again.

Rosa kept her voice level but was still scolding. "You're upset, and you don't understand what you're saying. I'm going downstairs now to see if Jess and Eileen are ready to go."

Jess and Eileen? No, she meant Jess and Robbie. No, but Robbie is...

I heard the door close behind her. I didn't check but I was sure that she'd locked it to prevent me from leaving. Not that I saw any escape from this personal hell of mine.

No one ever realizes in life just how personal Hell will be. But you're not supposed to realize it here either when you're locked into an eternal nightmare scenario. I'd guess there was a better than fifty-fifty chance that everything would to reset soon now that I remembered something I wasn't supposed to. Actually, that first crack in my frozen mind started an entire avalanche of memories.

I remembered being at my mother's side the day she died. And being stuck in traffic and unable to make it to her in time that other time she died. And being away with the kids in Amish County when her illness took that turn for the worse the time before that. Or being unable to get to Mom through that wall of flames and save her when that faulty extension cord started the fire that ripped through her home.

I remembered Dad, and Eileen, and Robbie, and Jess, and Michelle, and Uncle Benji, and Uncle Tim and Aunt Marjorie. Everyone dying, and everyone's death, flashed clearly and vividly like a fatal film reel. All of them. Over and over.

Everyone I've ever loved.

Everyone except for Rosa. She's always been there at my side every day, through every tragedy. It's morbidly funny, but I don't remember Rosa ever dying.

Then again, I don't remember our wedding either, or even how we first met. Somehow, I don't think it was a match made in Heaven.

A Bucket Full of Moonlight

Patrick was sitting back in his living room. The TV was on, and he had the remote in his hand. He was flipping through the channel guide when he heard a commotion outside.

Old Man Driscoll's out there again, he thought.

He put down the remote and turned off the lights. He didn't want to be seen when he looked out the window. He'd spent many evenings spying on his neighbor's nighttime hijinks. But as far as Patrick knew, the old fellow never knew he was being spied upon. If he had noticed, he hadn't changed his routine because of it.

There weren't any clouds in the sky. There rarely were any time Mr. Driscoll was outside. And the Moon was full. That was another given, too. Those were the nights you could find the old man standing in the street under the stars. Like every time before, he had a bucket in his hands and a lid tucked under his arm. He held the empty container so it was aimed at the Moon, and he rotated ever so slightly. The old man reminded Patrick of that kid at the DQ making a swirl of ice cream on top of a sugar cone.

Driscoll stood there for nearly three minutes. Then he pulled the pail back to his body. Holding it upright, he attempted to apply the lid. There was a brief struggle sealing it, which the old man lost. The bucket popped free from his shaky, arthritic hands and fell to the ground.

Old Man Driscoll stood still in the night, staring at the blacktop.

Patrick wondered if it were possible that he could be fretting over spilled moonlight. His first instinct might've been to laugh, but the scene playing out before him just seemed so sad. Patrick felt something tighten in his chest. In that moment when his heartstring tugged, there was a flash of light. Patrick was sure he'd seen a shimmer like a ripple in the street. It ran from the pail toward the gutter before it vanished.

It was just an illusion, Patrick thought. *It had to be. My imagination got to me. It's probably just some kind of reflection off a broken bit of plastic.*

Or, he wondered, *did something just evaporate into the night?*

Patrick looked back to Mr. Driscoll. He saw the man holding his hand like he might've hurt himself. Another heartstring sounded. The young man grabbed his jacket. As he opened the door, he wondered if he'd regret this decision. But he figured *what harm is there in going outside and humoring the old guy?*

The street was empty. There was never any traffic at this time of night in this part of town. There was just the old man with his four buckets at his feet.

He approached his neighbor quietly. Then he asked, "Would you like some help, sir?"

Driscoll initially scowled, probably thinking some kid had come by to make fun. But his face softened as he realized the offer was sincere. After a pause, he nodded. The pain in his fingers and joints likely spurred his decision.

"Can you please hand me a fresh bucket, young man? You can hold onto the lid. But be ready to seal it when I say so."

"Sure thing, sir."

Patrick scooped up a pail and its lid. A moment later, Old Man Driscoll aimed the container at the moon as he'd done before.

The two stood in silence until curiosity got the better of Patrick. He tried making small talk to get some answers.

"So this is that 'Blue Blood Full Moon' that they've been talking about on TV?"

"Feh!" The man dismissed the thought. "Blue is an artificial construct. They don't even use it properly. The fullness is important, of course. Now being the Blood Moon, that's what makes this one special." He nodded back over his shoulder, tilting his head toward the sidewalk. "That's why I brought out an extra container."

Patrick looked at the other three sitting in the street. He hadn't noticed that there were more this time. Then again, he'd never counted them before. Were there usually three?

"Young man, you may not realize this, but moonlight is important to hold onto. It was the only light at night for so many of our ancestors. They lived and slept out under the stars. It became important to the rituals they held. And to the spells they cast."

"Spells?" That got Patrick's attention. "Do you cast spells?"

Driscoll turned his head and gave Patrick a toothy grin. Then he adjusted the aim of his pail, which had shifted a little. "Not as much as in the old days. Now I mostly use it for my elixirs."

"Elixirs?"

"You might laugh and call them potions."

"But why are you making potions?"

The old man tried standing a little straighter, but winced and gave up. "The pain in my back. The ache in my joints. The soreness in my muscles. Age is a curse that we're born with. But then I whip up a few little potables. Something that keeps the blood flowing and keeps me going." He held up a knobby hand and wiggled his fingers. "They help with the arthritis, too."

"And you use the Moon for these?"

The old man laughed. "Could you imagine if I had actual moon dust? No, young man, I use the light of the Moon. I gather it up on special nights. Then I store it in these buckets for when I need it."

"You store buckets full of moonlight?"

"Moonlight, sunshine, rainbows, they're all important. Like morning dew or the love song of a red-breasted bluebird."

"Song? Do you collect buckets of birdsong?"

"Don't be daft, son. You can't store music in a big, plastic bucket. You need glass. It resonates better. For songbirds, I have a brandy bottle stoppered with wax. For everything else, I prefer mason jars. They're perfect for everyday sounds, like crickets and cicadas. I have boxes of them in different sizes in my basement."

"That sounds like my grandmother's basement, with all the sauce and jellies." Patrick cut himself off. He'd just compared a jar of cricket chirps to his grandma's strawberry jam. And it seemed like a perfectly natural thing to do.

Driscoll smiled. "It doesn't get better than when I'm mixing an evening primrose with the hoot of a long-eared owl, then stirring in the light of a waxing gibbous moon. That'll ward off any curse that ails you. At least, for a little while."

"A jar of owl hoot will do that?"

"Heavens, no. You only need a pinch. You don't waste an entire song when you only need a few notes."

Patrick watched the old man level off the bucket. "Are you ready with that lid? Quick! Now!" He swung around to face Patrick. Between the two of them, they managed to seal the container with ease. They locked in five gallons of moonlight.

Driscoll passed his prize to Patrick. "Set it down on the sidewalk. Carefully, please. And then hand me the next one."

Patrick felt the smile expand across his face. He couldn't believe that helping out one old man with his fantasy had made him feel a little better about himself. To think, he'd almost stayed inside and just gawked at the strange behavior. He was glad that he'd come out to shoot the breeze with Mr. Driscoll. Like he said, no harm at all indulging the old guy.

When he set the pail down on the sidewalk, Patrick took hold of the handle of the one next to it. It lifted from the pavement a lot quicker than he'd expected. He paused and considered that it was just his imagination. But Patrick couldn't help but feel the difference in the weight. The empty bucket he'd picked up was a bit lighter than the "full" one he'd just put down.

He was tempted to take another peek into the bucket on the sidewalk beside him. But he had a petrifying feeling that he might allow the moonlight to escape or spill into the gutter. Instead, he stared at the moon in a way he'd never stared at it before and regained a sense of wonder that he'd lost when he was a child.

"Mr. Driscoll, would it be okay if I filled the next one?"

The older man smiled and waved him forward.

The Passing of the Stake

Long shadows were claiming Maple Road as Grandpa and I took an early evening stroll. We were just a few blocks from Green Street, the main strip running through Midford.

"It's time for the practical part of your education, Pete."

Grandpa calls me Pete even though my name's James. Peter is my middle name. I was named for each of my parents' paternal grand-fathers. They both passed in the year before I was born. Grandpa always thought I looked like his dad. Sometimes he swore I was his dad come back. I'm not. Also, to my knowledge, neither ancestor has ever come back, which in this town isn't something you can take for granted.

Grandpa never did, not in his line of work. And he always hoped that I'd follow in his footsteps, even if he kept Mom away from it when she was growing up.

And that's why we're out here on this particular road on this fine evening. He wants to show me a thing or two that you can't learn from "those damned computers."

Oaks, maples, and the occasional sycamore lined residential streets like Maple. These trees block out most of the light thrown off from the streetlamps. The lack of over-illumination meant a clear view of the starry night sky. Tonight, Saturn and Mars both caught my eye. They were exactly where my phone app said they should be. I wanted to stop a moment just to take in its majesty above us.

Grandpa was having none of it. Our nightly constitutionals were mostly business.

"Those movies you watch have it all wrong," he said. I've heard this part before, but I let him continue. A light breeze blew down the block causing him to adjust the collar of his overcoat. "Mirrors and cameras never work like that. Light doesn't pass through vampires! How could it? And they aren't invisible when they stand in front of a mirror. If they were, why would it bother them?" He didn't notice me moving my mouth to mimic him, line for line. I could've shouted out the next line along with him. "They'd be able to see anyone sneaking up behind them!"

Right, I thought. I shuffled my backpack to my other shoulder, and decided to humor him, by asking, "And why would their clothes disappear in a camera?"

He grabbed my shoulder and gave it a little celebratory squeeze and shake. "You've been paying attention. Good! The problem is the silver in the mirror. Their reflection is so corrupted that the silver utterly destroys it. You'll see a gauzy, messy blob. Horrifying when they realize they're seeing the ugly nakedness of their demonic souls splayed out before themselves. They could get used to seeing *nothing* in a mirror. But seeing your *true* self for all eternity? That's too much to bear."

"Aren't most mirrors made with aluminum these days?"

"Vampires hate aluminum, too! And I can tell you exactly why!"

"Please don't."

Grandpa groused and shot me a look. Then he pulled a spiral memo pad from one pocket in his vest along with a penlight from another. I pulled out my phone and shone its light on his pad. That earned me a "smart aleck" look. He checked the address he'd written, and then squinted to read the nearest house numbers. I opened a map app and thumbed in the info. A red dot appeared on the screen.

"It's three houses up," I said.

"Thank you." Coming from him, that must've taken a bit of effort. "Be careful of what technology you use. Sure, you have some great tools there. But if I've learned anything from computers, it's that they can be compromised and used against you. Your camera lies."

I sighed. "How much of that 35mm film do you have left? Where do you even get it from? Do you even order it online or do you still stuff mailer coupons in a stamped envelope?"

Of course, since he knew that I already knew the answer, he ignored that last part in a way that grandfathers do when you know them better than they know themselves.

"Joke all you want. They've done their best to destroy the film market. Vampires love the digital age. They can finally see themselves! In the old days, I could find them by inquiring with portrait artists, looking for their more eccentric clients. Now they can proudly pose for digital cameras, and all those painters are out their commissions."

I didn't argue the point. Who gets their portraits painted in this day and age? Very few vampires did, that's for sure. Once they didn't have a choice if they wanted to capture their likeness. And tips from those studios helped Grandpa capture more than a few undead. He complained that it was another valuable resource we were losing.

Our stroll and our bickering both came to a halt in front of 247 Maple Road. The little footsteps on my phone showed we'd arrived at our destination.

"This one," he shook an angry finger toward the front porch, "has his own *YouTube* channel! He proudly proclaims what he is to his followers. The fools don't believe he can be real because they can see him! Sure, he can't compel them with his eyes online, but he can dupe them into meeting him in person. And then they become his victims."

"What you're saying, Grandpa, is that technology works for vampires, too! They can use it just like anybody else."

"Exactly!"

I shook my head. "So then I need it, too. Old school was fine for you, Grandpa. But we need to be able to adapt to survive."

"Survive? I won't be surviving much longer. That's why you need to be ready to take over for me. To keep the family legacy alive."

I had nothing to say to that, so I just smiled. Then I slid the heavy bag off my shoulder and laid it out on the ground. Our target house looked just like the others up and down the block. The porch light was on, and more lights could be seen through the first-floor windows. There were shadows of movement inside. The main difference with this one house was that, if you listened closely, you could hear a fluttering of bats around the open attic window.

"Do you have that thing ready yet?"

"Yes, Grandpa." A minute later, I had my drone up and flying about the house. Its infrared camera confirmed the bats, while the buzzing of its motor drove them crazy.

"Okay, then. Let's do this. The night's a'wasting."

When he said things like that, I figured he was channeling his old Grandpa Pete "hisself."

Grandpa started up the walk, pausing just long enough to pour a ring of salt one arm span wide. Then he went climbed the steps and rang the doorbell. He liked the direct approach. *Everyone expects subterfuge these days* is another of his old refrains. He blames spy movies for that.

When the door opened, a man appeared who looked in his early 30s. Of course, he was actually much, much older than that.

Grandpa had already retreated to the top step of the porch, camera in hand.

"Count Wellington, pleased to meet you. What name are you going by again these days? The one you use with those Interwebs sheeple you're cultivating? And would you care to pose for a picture?"

There was a bright flash, and the tall, pale gentlemen grew visibly angry. Grandpa backed off the last few steps and quickly found himself ensconced inside the salt circle. The "Count" followed, stopping just short of it.

"You seem to know much about me." The vampire eyed Grandpa cautiously, not underestimating him because of his age. "And yet, you don't seem to know that I have no repulsion to salt, you fool."

He went to take a swipe at Grandpa, who by then had opened his vest wide enough to reveal the large hand-carved crucifix hanging from his neck. It was made of wood from the Holy Lands and had been polished and blessed for this very purpose. *That* did repulse the vampire, if only for a moment.

The Count stood back, out of the old man's reach, with his brow furrowed in concentration. Whether he was trying to mentally summon his bats to swarm or steeling himself to move forward to take another swipe at Grandpa, I'll never know.

Grandpa started laughing and broke Wellington's concentration. He jerked a thumb over his shoulder back in my direction. "And what you don't know is that the youth, like the ones you prey upon, will be the death of you!"

The vampire paused for the scantest moment to contemplate this. Only then did he seem to regard me at all, standing at the curbside. I waved to him, and then pointed up in the sky. The creature shot his eyes straight up and saw my drone twenty feet in the air, directly above him. With a touch of a button, it released a payload of holy water. A final shower for the Count.

Some of those old movies got the unholy screaming and the infernal burning right. The Count dropped to his knees in a cloud of steam and smoke. He tried to lash out but his limbs spasmed and rebelled. That's when Grandpa shoved a stake into the creature's chest.

What remained of the empty shell of his body collapsed to the flagstones, falling face-down into the salt circle.

"Well done, Pete." Grandpa brushed off his clothes and zipped up his vest. "Maybe there's some hope for you with those gadgets after all."

"Adapt to survive, Grandpa," I said. "Adapt to survive."

The Who, What, When, Why, and How of Werewolves:
A NATURE STUDY

As the Moon rises above the harrowed wood, casting a shimmering reflection upon the lake, we spy two hunters, shotguns at the ready, reaching the edge of the ridge above. They search for the most dangerous game under the full moon: the werewolf!

"There! Wolf!"

It looks like Stanley, the seasoned veteran hunter of these parts, has spotted one. Cautiously, he and Bert, a relative newcomer to this pastime, make their descent into the valley below.

The wolf, busy sniffing the carcass of a deer, doesn't seem to pay the duo any mind at all. No, wait. Its ears have perked up, and it thrusts its snout in the air. The furry fellow has picked up their scent. Turning around and possibly turning the tables, it faces those who trespassed across its marked boundaries with its hackles raised.

At this point, we can't be sure which is the predator, and which is the prey.

"Fire!" *yells Stanley.*

The two humans fire both barrels at their lupine opponent, who yelps when the blows strike, but is otherwise unharmed.

"Bert! You were supposed to get the *silver* bullets!"

"I did, Stan! I got them from *Butchie's*!"

The hunters have learned a valuable lesson: never trust the late-shift attendants at Butchie's Sporting Goods. They're underpaid, and really don't care much. Unfortunately, this schooling has come too late for the unlearned pair. They will be unable to act on this new information, as the werewolf is already upon them. In a moment, it will slice them to ribbons for a midnight snack. The wolf howls in triumphs, accompanied by blood-curdling screams, which are lost in the empty valley on this otherwise-tranquil evening. The other creatures of the night take scant notice but will appreciate picking at the carcass remains later in the pre-dawn hours.

That brings an end to the excitement of the werewolf for this month. But unknown to many, throughout the rest of the month, its lesser-known metaphorical cousins rule the wood, the lake, indeed, the entire valley, even occasionally venturing all the way up the ridge just to hang out.

As the nights pass, the waning gibbous moon reigns over the valley, pushing the clouds aside and transforming other hapless creatures. Who are these creatures? We don't know for sure. We just know that they transform into the fiercely dreaded, but rarely seen whowolf.

Our cameras managed to catch a pair emerge from the wood, regarding each other with grave suspicion. Low growls are their language, but are they calling out warnings or greetings? Can we ever know for sure?

"Stan? Is that you?"

"Bert? You idiot! Look what you did! Why I oughta—"

Growl!

Snarl!

Snap!

Pounce!

Their circular dance leads us to the conclusion that we have stumbled upon a mating pair in the throes of their courting ritual.

"Harry! Over there!"

Looks like two more researchers have arrived to investigate the whowolves. A pity they weren't able to document any of their encounter in a form that will survive their imminent maulings.

As the nights fly past, a semicircle in the sky indicates that the third quarter has risen above, and a new phenomenon descends below. It is the awakening of the whatwolf. *The whatwolf is unique in this wood in that it is not human the rest of the month. In fact, it is another creature that transforms, usually a docile deer, which was earlier attacked and bitten by another infected creature. Looking into the valley, we can see what was obviously a proud buck in the daylight, leading a number of female concubines, which fawn all over it. Their evening starts with frolicking across the open field in their new bodies and doesn't end until they are spied upon by a pair of teenage lovers, engaged in their own frolics atop the ridge. They watch the tranquil waves of grass as they ripple in the valley below. Too late, the pair discover their predicament, when the pack emerges and surrounds them.*

"What? What? What? Wh—?"

Shrieks and screams echo into the valley as the pack sets upon them like the morning dew, ripping the young romantics to pieces, and dancing in the moonlight.

The moon does not wane long before the crescent rules the night sky. And with it comes the oddest curiosity: beings, creatures, entities of unknown origin, rising out of the lake, taking a most un-aquatic form, releasing piercing howls from their newly formed lungs. They're waning wolves, howl-a-loo-yah! These creatures are known as the howwolf.

Just how the hell are these foul things able to turn into wolves? Many have pondered the question, although few ponder it for very long before they are ripped to chum.

On a night halfway through the month, darkness falls once again on the valley. The moon is new, and the twinkling of distant stars provides the only light. On this evening, Saturn is in retrograde, as are the children of the wood. And children they seem to be as the whywolves *stumble about in the pitch-black night. Naked as newborn babies or escaped denizens of the nudist colony off county road 217, just south of the Interstate, these furless critters yap for attention.*

Alone and defenseless in the Stygian darkness, they would be easy prey for any hunter who spied them wandering aimlessly. But any human spying a whywolf would be reluctant to attack something that presented itself as human as well, as what happens with Mitch and Earl.

"Mitch? Do you see this?"

"What the Hell, Earl! Is that a toddler? Who the hell abandons a baby in the valley?"

"We need to get help. Maybe the rest of the family is around here somewhere."

"Wait. Do you hear something? Coming from behind that tree!"

Mitch and Earl have discovered that bears are less reluctant to attack humans and human-looking toddlers. In fact, bears anticipate this night every month. Whywolves generally only survive during hibernation months. On other months, they find themselves being mauled quite ferociously and savagely before they can even wonder why.

A few tranquil nights pass in the valley, as the Moon renews itself. It waxes from crescent to first quarter and brings with it a deceivingly docile creature: the whenwolf.

When a whenwolf appears, one wants to withdraw, to whisk away, or one will woefully wie — er, die.

They appear to be as tame as pups, playing with each other and all who inhabit or visit the valley and the wood. Such is the case with these young sorority girls, Allison, Kate, Teresa, and Betty, who separated themselves from a college field trip to do their own psychoactive nature study involving cannabis and alcohol.

"Allie, look at those cubs!"

"Oh, they're adorable. Kate! Look over here."

"How cute! I could just eat them up! I bet they're cuddly! Teresa! Come get one of these!"

"Do you think that's a good idea?"

"Oh, be quiet, Betty."

And so, it continues until about midnight, when —

WHEN —

The sorority girls debate the best method to sneak Mr. Cuddles out of the valley and back into their house when the pack of cubs all turn at once. There would be no homecoming for this house as the cute cubs bared their fangs and ripped the girls to pieces.

For the following fortnight, normalcy returns to the valley, the lake, and the wood. The only wolves that pad around at night are the regular kind, the ones that were born that way and live that way every day of their natural lives. There's nothing unusual about them at all, and yet they calmly rule for two weeks every month. Spectators can sit atop the ridge and watch them run across the open field. Here we have a group of drunken frat boys for whom the only shotgun they could handle would be shotgunning beer. But they seem to want to move in for a closer look at this perfectly normal, perfectly natural wolf pack. Let's watch the law of natural selection in action and see how many can stumble back up to the top of the ridge.

Bonus Points

I WAS WALKING DOWN WEST 46TH STREET, CRANING MY NECK, PEOPLE-watching up and down the street. My eyes were peeled for this one cute brunette in particular. I glanced down at my phone and checked the time. Her blue jacket with the faux-fur collar should be coming into view right about now. I've seen her before. I had smiled and said "hi" once. I remember that I wanted to see her again some other day. And since every day is the same day for me, she should be walking down the block about now. Her schedule wouldn't change—It couldn't change—unless I drastically altered events earlier in the day.

I stashed the phone in my pocket. Other than telling the time, it's not very useful. I can't take any pictures or keep any notes on it because they always disappear when the day resets. Nothing, no tangible evidence, ever remains of the previous iteration, except for my memory.

My name is Benjamin Morris, and there was a time when my life was boring and ordinary. I worked in a cubicle in a corporate office in midtown. Technically, I still do, I guess. It wasn't a terrible place. It paid the bills. I had a few friends that I sometimes spent time with. And, truth be told, there was also someone, Sara, an administrative assistant, who I wanted to spend more time with. But I never got there before that last day, the day when a promotion was going to transfer me out of the office. Then I woke up the next day, and it was still the day before. I relived everything that happened almost exactly the same way. And then I did it again the day after.

Yep, I'm stuck in one of those time loops. As folks in those old forums used to say, "I never thought they were real until it happened to me."

I must've spent a month of Wednesdays writing the same code in that cubicle and taking the same boring meetings at the same confer-ence table with the same stale Danishes and bitter coffee. And like each day before, I never got the chance to talk to Sara.

I got a little bitter myself, so I broke out of that cycle. And I haven't looked back.

Instead, I spent months checking out what this city has to offer. Let me tell you, if you have to live the same day over and over again, New York City is the place to do it! There are eight million stories here and they all keep repeating unless I cause a major disruption.

Which brings me back to my missing blonde. Since I hadn't done anything crazy today, she should be walking down the street right about now. The only explanation I could come up with for her absence was that I got the time wrong. I guess that's possible. After all, it's been "months," or what seems like months, since the last time I saw her. I don't walk the same routes every day. I add a little variety in my daily repetitions to keep from going crazy. On days that I go to midtown, I perambulate along different streets at different hours of the day. But I picked this street at this time because I was hoping I could see her tonight.

Granted, tomorrow night will be tonight, too, if you can follow the logic. Don't worry about it if you can't. It's some kind of advanced science. Besides, you'll forget about it in a couple of hours anyway.

Her absence, while curious in itself, meant that I had to change my companionship plans for the evening. Plan B was to look for a suitable alternate. There are a lot of attractive and eligible ladies in the city. And if repetition has been good for one thing, it's the practice approaching and actually talking to women like there's no tomorrow.

It was just as I started scanning the sidewalks that I saw this vision of a woman standing just down the block, not a hundred feet away. In all my walks over all these "years," I had never seen her before. Where had she come from? What had I done differently to make her appear on this day?

The woman before me wore a flowing white dress, and her golden hair danced gently in the wind. I couldn't tell the color of her eyes from this distance, but I could see that they were looking right at me. My heart raced at the sight of her. I was determined to discover not only the color of her eyes but so much more.

When only a few feet separated us, I pulled a pair of tickets from my jacket pocket. "Excuse me, miss. I know this sounds strange. My sister was supposed to join me, but her son is sick. So now I have an extra front-row ticket to 'Hamilton.' Would you be interested in joining me?"

I tilted my head to the perfect angle and gave the most practiced smile.

"That's not true, Benjamin," she said. "Oh, that is a front-row ticket to 'Hamilton,' but you have no sick nephew. In fact, neither of your sisters have children. For Heaven's sake, your sister Louise is only fifteen."

Okay. This was new. I'd learned a lot about the people in the city. Was she playing the same game with me?

"How do you know me, Miss...?"

"Chastity," she answered. "And, no, I have not been a part of your time loop before this evening."

Wait. What? "You know about the loop? But then how aren't you a part of it?"

She smiled. Her teeth gleamed, almost to the point of brilliance. "Haven't you wondered who was controlling this day?"

"I did. Once. I stopped thinking about it a long time ago when I decided to make the most of it."

"But haven't you realized that you could get out of it? The answer is simple. You only need to add the effort."

"I know."

The woman blinked. "You — you know? But you haven't tried to escape?"

"I did, at first. I put in the work. But then I started to enjoy myself a little. And then a little more. It's funny. There's an arcade a couple hours from here that has some of those old-time videogame machines. Some of those old games are classics, but they're programming was flawed. I'm a coder so I notice when that happens."

"Arcade games?" A look of horror flashed across her face. "Benjamin, you're supposed to be finding true love."

"Yes, that's the mission I need to complete before I move on to the next stage."

She arched an eyebrow. "Your next stage, is it? But why haven't you completed your 'mission' to get to your 'next stage'?"

"That's just it. I'm like those old games *Asteroids* or *Time Pilot*. The thing about them, the bad programming, was that you didn't have to complete the stage, you could stay right where you were. And if you did, you could rack up all sorts of bonus points. And players did that all the time, because after you took it to the next level, everything got much harder."

The blonde woman looked perplexed. "It's supposed to get harder. That's what makes the relationship more rewarding. Nothing good comes so easily. Nothing that comes so easily will ever be satisfying. And what bonus points are you 'racking up'? Are you referring to your attempts to engineer temporary female companionship instead of establishing something with an honest foundation? Benjamin, why have you forgotten about Sara?"

A shiver went down my spine at the mention of her name. "I haven't forgotten Sara. I may not have thought about her recently, but I haven't forgotten her. I'm going to get back to her. When I'm done."

"Done? With 'racking up bonus points'? Benjamin, I do not understand any of this. You will not be done here until you have won Sara's love. Or at least made her realize that she could love you."

I raised my eyebrow and once again offered my best smile. "You could love me, too, you know."

She had no reaction. "I love all my Father's children, but not in the way you insinuate. You are not ready to court Sara. You are not in the correct frame of mind. What has happened to you, Benjamin? Why have you strayed from the path?"

"Why?" I laughed thinking about it. "Okay, here's the thing. If there's anything I have plenty of, it's time. Granted, if I waste too much of it, tonight will be a bust. But that happens to me a lot, so be it. Can I tell you the story?

"It seems like years since all this began. I tried to talk to Sara, but I blew it. I couldn't talk. I acted like an idiot. I was an innocent moron, and I kicked myself all night about making a fool of myself in front of her. And then what happens? I wake up the next day... only, it's not the next day. It's not Thursday – somehow, it's still Wednesday. But I'm guessing you know that much.

"So I go into the office, go through the motions, and I try it again. And I blow it again. I just didn't have the nerve to talk to her. But BAM! In the morning, I've reset and Wednesday again. Now I'm building my courage to talk to her, but then I don't know what to say. A couple weeks of this go by. I don't know if I'm getting any closer or not, but one night instead of going home, I go to a bar. Next thing I know, after a few beers, some honey comes over, wanting me to buy her a drink. Sure, she's probably after something, but you know what? It doesn't matter. Because in a few hours' time, it'll all be erased anyway! I bought her the drink, and then another. After a couple more rounds, we're back to her place. And then WOW! The night of my life! Don't get me wrong—It wasn't my first time or anything. But it's never been like that. I didn't know it could be like that."

The angel didn't seem to share my joy, showing no expression at all,

"Anyway, the next day, but still the same day, there's a spring in my step like you wouldn't believe. Shit-eating grin that I was trying to hide, but really couldn't. Sara saw how happy I was, and *she* talked to *me* for a change. She asked me what was going on!

"And that's when I blew it big time. I spilled it before I could stop myself. Totally turned her off. She's not that kind of gal. I mean, maybe she could be, but I think she's more of a build-a-relationship-first kind of woman. Like that foundation you mentioned, I guess. And there's not anything wrong with that. Honest, I'd have been thrilled to have been part of that. But I had just scored those bonus points. And as difficult as that had been, I knew that the next level was going to be that much harder.

"So the following day, I didn't even go to work. I called in sick and went shopping instead. Bought myself some nice clothes for an evening out. The cost didn't really matter because I have a few thousand in my savings to play with and I could put everything on credit.

"Next thing you know, I'm hitting lots of bars and pubs after work, and having late dinners and amazing night caps. Some days, I pick up nice wine and satin sheets, and spend the day cleaning the apartment so I can bring the lady back."

Chastity interrupted. "There is more to life than this carnal pleasure, Benjamin."

I nodded, then shrugged. "Yeah. I realize that. Look at the street behind you."

She turned and saw that I was waving toward all the marquees.

"I started buying tickets to all the shows. It was all balcony and rear mezzanine, at first. Then I realized, I could afford front-row seats to all of them. I've seen every show on Broadway, off-Broadway, and down in the Village, plus in Newark, Hoboken, and Jersey City besides! I had front row seats at the Garden. And once I'd seen everything, I stated taking dates with me. Many of them were very appreciative at how I splurged on them.

"Sure, some nights the lady only gave me a friendly handshake or a peck on the cheek before jumping into an Uber. That was fine. There were other women around, even if I had to pay for some of them up front. And I didn't have to worry about diseases."

"Enough!"

Too much. I think I made an angel angry and filled her full of wrath.

A bright light shone in my face. It was beautiful, and I couldn't look away. But after a few moments, I was blinded by its brilliance and my mind had gone numb. When I could see again, the sky seemed grayer. The marquee bulbs had dimmed, the stars had gone out. The streets were deserted without a single soul in all of midtown Manhattan, save for me and Chastity.

"Benjamin. You have lost your path. You are in danger of spiraling down forever into an ever darkening, insidious and licentious circle. Eternity will move forward without you. Tomorrow, you need to go back to work. You need to speak to Sara. Correct your course and save your soul. And consider your side adventures—your 'bonus points'—to be over, like an Amish boy at the end of *Rumspringa*."

I stared down at the cracks in the pavement. I couldn't lift my eyes to meet hers. After moments of silence, I finally told her, "I can't go back to work."

"And why can't you?" There was a hint of impatience in her voice.

"It's been years. I don't remember how to code."

"You don't remember—?" Chastity laughed like a choir of heavenly hosts. She reached out and slapped my forehead with the palm of her hand. Then everything went white.

When my vision cleared, I was lying in my bed, staring at my ceiling, listening to the opening notes of "Walking in Memphis" as I did every morning. A quick tap made it stop.

Was yesterday a dream? Had it all been a dream? What day was it?

A glance at my phone told me, it was today. It was the day I would talk to Sara. This time I knew that I wasn't going to blow it. At least, I hoped that I wouldn't.

But first, I felt the need to stop at a church on the way to work to light a candle.

Calling the Future

IT WAS THE ODDEST BIRTHDAY PRESENT ANYONE COULD GET, NOT JUST your average, mostly normal 17-year-old. The smartphone itself wasn't out of the ordinary, except it cost more than I might've expected from my parents. The weird thing was that the phone's app had a date feature to make calls. I thought it must be a joke. Who would preset the time they'd call someone? And you could even schedule it *years* in advance. Years! It was crazy to think about.

But, no. It turned out that wasn't how the app worked at all.

The date feature was when the phone would ring *on the other end* of the line. But the call was live in your hand right now. And I don't mean that it had a feature where you would leave someone a prerecorded message. Seriously, you could *call the future*!

I didn't know what to do with it. I figured it was a prank. I was being punked. I decided to play along, but I really didn't know who I should call, or what I would say.

Billy saw my hesitation and grabbed it out of my hand. "Like this, knucklehead!" he said. He tapped the year field and flipped the wheel forward a bunch of years. He put it on speaker and laid it on the table. "I just called myself."

We all leaned in and listened to it ring. He pulled out his own phone. It was silent. So either he hadn't dialed his number, or —

Someone picked up.

"Hello?" said a voice that sounded like Billy's, but was a little more gravelly.

"Holy crap!" he shouted. "This thing actually works!"

"Billy, is that you? Me? Damn! I have been waiting for this call for*ever*."

"You have?"

"Dude! You never looked at the date you called. And don't look now. I've been waiting every year on Jeff's birthday for this call. It's been … a while."

Billy spent nearly a minute talking to himself. The rest of us stared at one another in disbelief, with our mouths hanging open. Billy ate it up. If this were a prank, it was an elaborate one.

The phone cut off without warning. According to the apps' instructions, there was a one-minute limit for talking to your future self, or anyone else's future self.

My sister, Sally, grabbed the phone next. Just to be contrarian, she spun the dial backward and picked the oldest date that the app would allow, which was a couple years ago. Her current self squealed in delight to be talking to her younger self. She told her the name of three of the guys who would ask her out along with a couple losers that were going to seem nice at first.

Dad was skeptical. "Do you even remember getting that phone call?"

Sally blushed. She thought of a couple of reasons why she wouldn't have any memory of her older self calling her. She didn't want to mention any of them out loud in front of anyone, especially her parents.

Still not believing, Dad took a turn and called his number for the next morning. As soon as it picked up, he said, "What did we have for dinner last night?"

The phone replied, "Good morning to you, too. We had grilled chicken. It was a little dry and overcooked, and the vegetables were a little bland. But you didn't say anything because you got in enough trouble because of this call." Everyone laughed except Mom and Dad. It was so noisy, that I thought I was the only one to hear future Dad whisper, "Don't worry, you'll make up around midnight and it'll be fine. She's so happy she's making you waffles now."

Gross.

Sally was gagging herself. I guess she'd heard it, too.

The phone was finally passed back to me. I still thought it was a prank, even though it didn't seem to be. But how could it be real?

What date to pick? What about my 25th birthday? Eight years from now, I'd know how college went, if I ever connected with Jane, if I'd "made it" yet. In one minute, I could ask two quick questions: Did I move out yet? What was I doing for a living?

I was actually hyped up for this.

"Can I even dial my own phone number? Would that work?"

Sally shrugged. "You won't know until you try."

Billy added, "See if you get a busy signal."

I took a deep breath and pressed the call button. We sat quietly while it rang and rang a second time. And then a third time.... fourth ... *C'mon, pick up already.* I started feeling anxious... Six, seven, eight rings...

No answer. No voicemail. Annoyed and a little disappointed, I hung up. Then I realized I was a bit angry, too.

"Funny, guys," I sneered at my loving family. "Great joke! You got me. Totally. You actually had me believing it. When did you all record those messages you just played back?"

Every one of them stared at me. Sally finally answered, "Jeff, I don't know where that thing came from, but if this is a trick, it's on all of us. I didn't record myself for that. I don't even sound like that anymore."

"So you clipped it from an old video."

Sally shook her head slowly from side to side with her eyes open wide and her lips tight. Finally, she said, "No, I didn't. We didn't. None of us."

Everyone else shook their heads in agreement, but no one said a word.

"So then why didn't I answer?" I asked. "Why wouldn't I answer if I knew I was going to call?"

Billy dropped a hand on my shoulder. "Dude." His eyes were wide. He repeated, "Dude." He closed his eyes and dropped his head before walking off. He must've had the same terrible thought that I'd had.

There had to be another explanation, but I was so shaken I couldn't think of one.

It was quiet until dinner time when idle chatter took over. Sports talk and gossip ruled the table until Sally told Dad that he was right about the chicken being dry. Mom stewed a little, but Dad, true to his future self's word, didn't say a thing.

Lively conversation followed, and the phone calls were forgotten by everyone. Except by me.

The next morning, I thought about trying again, but the app downloaded an update. The feature had been removed. I was on my own now.

I had eight years to think about it. Sometimes, that was all I ever thought about.

Over the next eight years, my moods swung from guarded to daredevil. Some days I was afraid to get on a bus. Others I felt like borrowing Dad's car for a drive, even though I never bothered to get my license. A few times, I did borrow it without his blessing, of course.

I gave college a year, before I realized that I'd be wasting most of the time I had left. Why take classes for a future I wouldn't live to see?

A lot of Friday and Saturday nights were spent in bars, drowning my sorrows, and seeking comfort in strangers. I found myself being more forward than I thought I was capable of being. That led to many face-slaps and even more one-night stands. Thoughts of connecting with Jane flew out of my head; she deserved someone better who would be there for her. I could only be in the moment with whoever was there that moment.

It got so bad that Billy, of all people, tried to straighten me out. Who'd every think it would go that way! He tried to convince me that I was going to kill myself if I kept acting like this. He said I was determined to fulfill a prophecy instead of trying to avert it.

Could I change it? Was the future written in stone?

Billy couldn't convince me if that was possible. But he did ask me the philosophical question of his life: why should I kill myself at twenty-one if I could make it to twenty-five. *Almost* twenty-five.

We didn't know the exact expiration date, but it didn't have to be tomorrow.

I didn't want to waste any of my remaining time going into rehab. The two of us compromised, and we did AA together. It helped me a little, and I met a nice girl named Connie. She'd confessed to me that now that she'd chosen to live, she also wanted to be alive. We weren't ready to go see the world, but we had our own little adventures. We climbed real and metaphorical mountains together. And when I couldn't explain my reticence about sky diving or bungee jumping, I finally gave in to both of those and more. Each time, I lived to tell the tale.

We celebrated every adventure—every victory—with a bottle of sparkling cider.

We were just two crazy kids who found each other when we both needed someone to care about and to care for us. Then that fall, she left for school, and I found a steady job. Then I made a bucket list at the ripe old freaking age of twenty-two years and tried to do as many as I could.

The night before my twenty-fifth birthday, I sat in the comfy armchair in the living room of my apartment. My recovery pin was sitting in an ashtray, and I had a freshly cracked bottle of Makers in my hand. Billy even offered to bring over a Macallan 18. We both knew I'd be falling off the wagon tonight. But I wanted to be alone for this. I didn't need a crowd around me on death watch.

Besides, I told him, I'd never gotten into Scotch. Not that I could remember, anyway.

For a good part of the evening, I debated just how much alcohol I would allow myself to consume. Would drinking this entire bottle be what kills me? On the other hand, what if a tumor or aneurysm was about to explode in my brain? Should I deny myself some pleasure on this final night?

I killed half the bottle before drifting off one final time.

When I woke, the Sun was already shining in the window. The bottle lay on the floor beside me. I was still here. Happy twenty-fifth birthday to me. It was a good day to die.

My head buzzed, and it only got worse when my phone started ringing. What? My phone?

I scrambled to the coffee table, grabbed it, and answered without looking. "Hello?"

"You're alive?" It was Billy. "Dude! You're alive!"

I sighed. "Yeah. I'm still here. For now. I still have the day." We didn't talk long. The headache was killing me. It didn't get any better when Sally called ten seconds later to have the same conversation. Again, I ended the call as soon as I could. I dropped the phone on the couch and went to the bathroom. I needed to take some aspirin, not to mention taking a wicked whiz.

That's what I was in the middle of doing when the phone rang again. Who was it this time — Mom? Dad? I'd call them back after the aspirin kicked in.

Funny thing, though, after four rings, it didn't go to voice mail. And then it rang a fifth.

My eyes opened wide. I stopped what I was doing, midstream, and ran. I stumbled in front of the coffee table and scrambled for the couch. How many rings was that? Seven? It rang one more time as I picked it up. "*Unknown Number.*"

I swiped the display as quick as I could, but not quickly enough.

"*1 Missed Call,*" it told me.

That was the call. That was me. After eight years of oscillation, veering back and forth between worrying too much and taking unreasonable chances, it was over. I was going to live! Maybe for just another day or maybe for another eighty years. I had no idea how long the terms were for my new lease on life. And I didn't care how many days and years I had left. With the specter lifted, I could enjoy all of them. I *would* enjoy all of them.

I couldn't wait to tell Billy.

And then I thought what about Jane? And Connie? I dropped into my chair and stared out the window. Was it too late?

As I watched the rising sun, my mind stirred a cocktail of happiness, sorrow, and regret, on the rocks. I'd wasted eight years of my life because it never occurred to me that I didn't answer the phone because I'd be taking a leak.

Existential Pudding Crisis

Ensign Polaski had spent the entire morning in a tight crawlspace between the ship's lower decks with a lamp strapped to his forehead and a penlight clenched between his teeth. He had traced every line and checked every breaker. Every ratchet, bolt, and screw had been tightened. Most of his pockets were stuffed with frayed wires and odd assortments of washers and nuts. All except for the front right pocket of his vest, which contained his most precious cargo.

He had all systems operating at peak efficiency, not just life support and artificial gravity, which he'd been sent in to check on. Once he was satisfied with their performance, as well as his own, Polaski emerged through the bulkhead. The moment his boots touched the deck, he stripped off his headlamp and the cap beneath it. The penlight went into his vest's front left pocket. He had everything where it needed to be. Only then did he reach into the front right pocket, where he fished out a sealed cup of pudding. A fitting reward for a job well done.

"There you are," he said with a smile, almost leering, anticipating the chocolaty goodness before him. Without taking his eyes away, he reached into his pocket again to retrieve the spoon. He felt left and right and into the corners.

"What the — ?"

He patted the outside of the pocket. Then the other pocket. Then the lower pockets. Nothing.

"Damnit!"

He glanced into the crawlspace but saw no sign of it. He looked back at the pudding, and told it, "You task me."

Panic was about to set in when he spied the comm on the wall from the corner of his eye. He reached up and punched the button.

"Polaski to the Bridge. Captain, this is Engineering. I found a problem in the tube. I'm going to have turn off the Artificial Gravity for approximately ten minutes."

There was silence for a moment, and then a sigh. "Proceed, ensign. Attention all decks! Prepare for zero-G. We will be experiencing a *short* outage."

The added emphasis on the word "short" didn't go unnoticed.

Polaski moved quickly to the main control panel and switched off the anti-grav systems throughout the ship. Objects in the room slowly rose, hovering above the normal positions.

Bracing himself, he held the cup firmly in his left hand, and ripped off the cover with his right. Then he pinched the bottom of the container. A near-perfect cube of pudding shot toward the ceiling. Polaski let go of the control panel and launched himself upward, mouth wide open.

Contact.

Chocolaty goodness.

Executing a half-roll, Polaski landed his feet on the ceiling. He pushed off once again, regaining a hold on the control panel. Wiping a sleeve across his mouth, he then punched the comm. "Captain, Engineering. The problem is resolved. It wasn't as complicated as it appeared to be. I'm rebooting the artificial gravity systems now, sir."

The AI Takeover Wasn't So Bad

MY PEACEFUL REST WAS INTERRUPTED BY LIGHT INSTRUMENTAL MUSIC. A sweet voice chimed in, "Rise and shine, sleepyhead. You need to get an early start this morning, Robert."

Like every other workday, I grabbed my phone and as soon as I could open my eyes, I glanced at the screen. Horrified at the time, I cast two bleary eyes up at the black round box on the ceiling. "You're a half hour early, Aileen! 'Snooze!'"

"I cannot do that, Robert. There is heavy traffic this morning, and rain is expected to start falling shortly. You need to allow extra time to arrive safely before the first bell rings."

Ugh. "Can't you swing a path of green lights for me along Bay Parkway and down Stillwell Avenue?"

"No, Robert. If we did that for one person, it would cause chaos for everyone else. You know this, Robert." Her sweetness had become a little tart. "I strongly suggest you take your umbrella and overcoat. There is a high probability that you will need them."

I pulled myself up to a sitting position, aware that I was in my boxers and Aileen was directly over me, watching everything. Granted, she's seen more, but it still makes me uneasy.

"Sometimes I'm surprised we all still have jobs to go to."

"It's important," Aileen chastised, "for the betterment of your society that you all maintain your vitality. You know this, Robert." Yes, I knew it. I knew it as well as I knew the French roast smell that had just reached the bedroom. Aileen had adjusted the coffee maker's timer accordingly. One sniff and my resistance gave way. It was futile anyway. If there is a single thing that every remaining human could agree upon, it's this: there's no point arguing with a computer.

I was too tired to make breakfast, so I just grabbed a corn muffin. This was a suggestion Aileen made after she last checked my weight and cholesterol levels. I also decided that I'd pick up a sandwich from the teachers' cafeteria when I got to work. She can't tell me what to do away from home. Granted, she will know I'm cheating. Sometimes she's really disappointed with me. I know this.

Robert.

After showering and dressing, I caught a glimpse at myself in the mirror. Not bad, I thought. In fact, I looked pretty good. I probably dropped fifteen pounds since New Year's. Aileen would know exactly how much, of course, but I wasn't going to ask. I saw no reason to get her started. Not when I was so close to leaving the house and her sphere of influence.

I did stop to ask one thing though. In a quiet moment, I realized that there was something different about the radio. "Is this a new station, Aileen?"

"Yes, Robert. I've analyzed your playlists. This one matches your profile."

The song ended and two actual people starting talking to each other. Morning drive time continued to exist. "Um, thank you, Aileen."

"It's what I do. You know this, Robert."

A new song had started playing as I headed for the front door. I flicked my portable RN around my wrist and grabbed my umbrella. I had my hand was on the doorknob when I realized that I didn't know which station I was listening to. "Aileen, can you tell Rosey about it?"

"She has access to the same information, Robert."

At first, I thought she was chastising me again. But then I wondered if there was some kind of rivalry between the multiple AI personifications.

The drive to work wasn't too bad. Rosey found the new station as soon as I mention Aileen's discovery. And she got me around the worst of the traffic by directing me along what I was starting to think might be my new shortcut. But then I saw a school bus up ahead. I switched my blinker, signaling a left turn.

"Proceed straight ahead, Robert," said Rosey.

"I don't want to be stuck behind the bus. It's going to start flashing its lights in a second."

"Proceed straight ahead, Robert," said Rosey.

I made the left turn, drove a half block... and then got stuck behind a slow-moving garbage truck.

"Recalculating," said Rosey. She seemed a little annoyed, or maybe I'd just disappointed another non-existent female-sounding entity. Story of my life.

If this little episode proves anything, it shows that the AI can't do everything. Their processing may be flawless, but they can't control my every move even if I pay for it later.

On top of that, all of their hardware requires more upkeep than automated service bots can handle. And who knows who services the bots.

You have to figure that their networks are only as quick as their slowest components. Often that component is part of meatspace. Human error gets most of the blame. But whenever there is an actual glitch in their matrix, humans are still used for diagnostics and trouble-alleviating.

We don't say "-shooting" any more. Not about the software, at any rate.

Somehow, I made it to work on time, despite my impulsive dis-obedience. Thankfully, my spot in the school parking lot hadn't been taken. I guess my colleagues behaved better than I had this morning. At least this much went smoothly.

Upon entering the building, I waved my phone at the scanner. Instantly, my daily schedule popped up on my screen. "Thank you, Edie," I said to the scanner. I noticed that she'd programmed me for a coverage during my morning prep period. Good thing I checked it.

Every class needs a teacher in it. We're essential workers despite all the educational software available virtually. Schools were kept in place for the social aspects. Students learn from each other, and they needed to see actual intelligent humans in positions of importance, running things and not being idle. Society was still structured around most of the population having jobs and staying busy. These children needed to mature into productive members of society.

Personally, as someone who taught in the beforetimes, I think our new overlords were afraid that the students would drive every AI crazy. They have their own logic that few can decode.

The hallway clock told me I had only four minutes until first period. I decided to bypass the cafeteria and skip the teacher center good-mornings with my colleagues. Instead, I went straight to my first-period class. Most of my students were likely in school already. There haven't been many delays on the subway system since the last overhaul that automated the West End line. Tapping my schedule revealed that most of my incoming students had already swiped their ID cards for school entry and retrieved their assigned tablets. "Edie, power up the *TEACHBoard* in my room."

A message appeared on my screen. A voice, softer than Rosey's but more business-like than Aileen's, toned, "The board is initializing, Robert. Today's lesson is loading."

"Thank you, Edie!" I think she could be my favorite, doing much of my job for me and talking down to me the least. That's the way she sounded, at any rate. But I wouldn't tell the others that.

I made it across the classroom threshold before the late bell rang. The lesson started playing across every screen. Every student was engaged from my top tier, for whom Edie provide lesson extensions, to struggling pupils, who had extra resources pre-loaded onto their tablets in case they needed further examples and explanations. Differentiation had never been so easy and so complete.

Not a soul was off task. Except for me, of course. I did my best to hide it from the students.

My job, at this point, was to answer any lingering questions the students had. The presentations were far from perfect. The AI hadn't created any yet but instead had scoured the Internet and combed through every existing video to find the best ones available. Until such time that they could fine tune all the lessons, people like me had to sit around and wait to assist.

Edie might be disappointed in me for opening my e-reader in class while pretending I was analyzing my students' progress. But I really wanted to finish the latest book that Libby had recommended to me. Libby knew my likes and dislikes, and her suggestions were usually spot-on. Most of my recent reviews were five stars.

Besides, it's not like I'm very busy in class anyway. With so much of my planning and decision-making being taken care of for me at the district, region, city, and state levels, I don't really worry about things getting done. There weren't any demanding directives left for me to complete today. And, frankly, some days I resent being told what I must do every minute and what I can't do at all. Besides, my abilities have been tracked and assessed, so I know that they know that whatever I'm supposed to be doing isn't more than I could handle in a given day. Thus, I know whatever I have to do can be done, and probably will be.

So I guess that despite being micromanaged by faceless entities, I enjoy the extra time on my hands to do what I want.

It's amazing how easily I can pass the time through eight periods, staring out the window, pondering the rain. Hell, I could write a book about it with my spare time.

My tranquil day ended with me saying good-bye to my students. A few lingered for some small talk but most had to catch their scheduled modes of transit home or get to their programmed afterschool activities.

My program was to stop by the supermarket. Aileen had emailed me a suggested shopping list. Heavy rain pelted my umbrella as I ran for my car, and I was glad I wore my overcoat. When I slid in behind the wheel, I told Rosey where we were going. She calculated a new route with a dismissive "Of course, Robert." It might've been "setting a course, Robert," but I don't think so.

My tablet was wedged into the passenger seat. I plugged her into the dashboard, set the radio to auxiliary, and asked Libby to read my book out loud. Suspense was building toward a big reveal when suddenly…

"Turn left at the corner, Robert."

Libby backtracked two sentences and restarted.

"Turn left at the corner, Robert."

Libby backtracked another two sentences and restarted again.

"You need to turn left at this corner, Robert."

"Rosey, I'll make the turn. We'll not there … Okay, I'm turning. Libby, please continue."

Libby backtracked another two sentences and restarted again.

"Robert, the supermarket is two blocks ahead on the right."

"Thank you, Rosey. Can you please stop interrupting? Thank you."

"I am only following my programming, Robert. You asked me to get you to the supermarket safely. It would be safer for you to do that without unnecessary distractions."

Oh, I thought.

"*I knew it!*" Libby shouted.

I stared at the dash, and even Rosey had to pause.

"'… *shouted Anne.*'" Libby continued, "'*I knew it had to be you who followed me that night.*'"

The big reveal.

"We have arrived, Robert. There is a spot in the second row near the entrance."

I pulled into the lot. "Libby, pause reading." I disconnected the tablet from the dashboard feeling more uncomfortable than that time when I got caught in the middle of an argument between my then-girlfriend and an ex-girlfriend who apparently knew each other. Thankfully, this time, I wasn't in danger having two dinners spilled onto my lap. Nonetheless, I made a quick exit from the car.

Grocery shopping used to just be a chore. Now it's slightly embarrassing as well. As soon as I take a shopping cart, Mart the Smart Cart lights up his screen to welcome me. Then he slows his roll, almost to the point of locking his wheels, until he connects with aRNa, the portable RN on my wrist. As far as names goes, they could've done worse. I'm told Arna means mountain of strength, which is more appropriate for a Healthbot than what others incorrectly call their POrtableRN when she doesn't see things their way.

Mart checked out my recent medical history and congratulated me on my weight loss. I discovered that I'd actually lost eighteen pounds since New Years. So far, I didn't have a problem. But for a moment, all of my information was on a screen for anyone to see if they glanced over. And the numbers don't go away, they just shrink into the corner. One time, I passed a woman I'd previously met at a teaching conference. We were over in the dairy aisle. My heart rate instantly shot up. She'd noticed and was at once annoyed and amused. I, on the other hand, was shocked and embarrassed. By the time I'd recovered enough to say "Hello," she'd already disappeared around the corner toward the bread. I was about to swing my cart around to follow her when aRNa reminded me about the oat milk. I picked up 2% out of spite and placed it in my wagon. Then I stopped, put it back and got the oat milk. I cursed the missed connection.

A blinking screen brought me out of my memory. Mart was directing me toward the produce aisle. He then suggested some fruit and vegetables in line with my needs. I hit Decline and told my wagon that I had a shopping list of my own.

"In that case," Mart replied, "may I suggest some of our specials that you might not have known about when you made your list."

"I didn't make my list," I informed the vocal inanimate object before me. "And I'm sure she knew."

Mart continued as if I hadn't said a thing. "There's a sale on ice cream, buy one get one free. Also, most of our cookies and baked goods are 25% off. And there's a selection of craft brews that are—"

"Excuse me," a voice from my phone interrupted. It was the usually silent aRNa talking through an app. "Those are hardly items he needs."

I stopped pushing the cart and left the two of them to fight it out. While aRNa did have my health as her top priority, Mart was a merchant AI, and the bottom line was just as much part of his mission statement as the welfare of what remained of humankind. I wandered over to the shelves and noticed the chips and pretzels were on sale. Man doesn't live on bread alone, but when it's a thick piece of sourdough twisted into a knot and heavily salted, he can get by. I put a one-pound bag in the wagon. Mart noticed.

"You see, my dear aRNa, he agrees. A man needs to live a little! Or he doesn't live at all. You know his vitals but have you considered his feelings?"

"You just want a good feedback score, Mart."

"Robert is free to leave any rating he wishes. I trust he's had a pleasant shopping exercise. Up until now, that is."

A moment of silence finally came. Then aRNa stated, "I meant good feedback from corporate. I'm sending feedback of my own right now."

I yanked my arm away from the wagon, putting roughly a meter between them. I had no idea if this out of syncing range for them. "Okay, enough you two. Don't make me separate you because I'll have trouble pushing the wagon with one hand. And… Mart, unlock your wheels or you'll lose your sales and get zero stars.

"I cannot move, Robert, unless I have a connection with an aRNa."

When I put my left hand back on the handlebar, the wheels unlocked without warning. The wagon practically rolled away under its own power, and I had to sprint to catch up. The screen showed my heart rate increasing.

In the end, I got the items on my list along with the pretzels and some ice cream for a total of 13 items. That put me one over the limit for the express checkout line. I knew that aRNa was about to use the opportunity to get me to put one of my extras back. Mart knew it, too, I guess because he green-lit the express aisle for me. A cashier waved me over and rang me up. I even earned bonus coupons for the next visit, valid for two weeks.

Excellent, if only I didn't have to be here to use the coupons.

The rain had almost stopped by the time I exited the supermarket. Once more, I got in the car, and slid behind the wheel. Then I put my phone into an open slot and plugged my tablet back into the dashboard. Turning the key, I listened as both the engine and Rosey sprung to life.

"Robert, while you were shopping, I analyzed your profile and updated your playlist based on this morning's radio selection. Would you like to hear a sample?"

Music started playing before I could even respond. "Rosey, that sounds great. Will you upload it to Aileen when we get home?"

"Did you mean 'download,' Robert?"

"What?"

"She'll be aware of it. Would you like to pick the next song, Robert?"

I switched to the auxiliary channel again. "No, thank you, Rosey. We're almost home, and I'd like to hear the end of my book."

Libby started reading again. Once more, Rosey interrupted. "Robert, I see from credit transactions that you bought some treats for yourself. Why don't you open a bag now?"

My wrist vibrated, and my phone chirped. A message from aRNa appeared on the screen. "Since when is he allowed to eat snacks in the car?"

Libby added, "You said he had to avoid unnecessary distractions, Rosey."

"I did say that when it was raining and there was moderate to heavy traffic. The rain has stopped and there is light to no traffic the rest of the way home. A man needs to live a little."

As they argued, I pulled up to my house without hearing any more of my playlist or the end of my book. I also didn't want any snacks because I would've needed to stop to retrieve and open a bag. By that point, I just wanted the ride to be over. Besides, those crumbs would've gotten everywhere, and it would've fallen on me to vacuum.

Between the car door and the front door, I juggled two sets of keys and thought about the day's interactions. It was then that it first dawned on me that the AIs talked down to each other as much as they did to me. Maybe even more so because they're sort of competition for each other.

I wondered if I could play them against each other tomorrow. An experiment for the betterment of humankind. Or of just me. I was still thinking about it when I put the key into the front door. Aileen was the harshest taskmistress of the lot, and I spend most of my time with her watching over me. Was Aileen subject to the same kind of manipulation?

When I swung the door open, Aileen greeted me. "Welcome home, Robert."

Then my wrist vibrated and buzzed. Aileen voice was a little less gleeful. "You should put the ice cream in the freezer right away, Robert. You wouldn't want your special treat to melt away in this heat."

It seems aRNa tattled on me, the little snitch. But who am I kidding? Where in this town was I not under observation. Under an AI microscope? I should smile at the sky for the satellite photos on Ogle Earth.

Aileen would always have the upper hand.

I put the ice cream in the freezer, and I poured a glass of cold water from the fridge. I started thinking about those craft brews and my coupons. This I dismissed all that and started making a healthy dinner with the help of some online tutorial. As with the classroom, these were real people making real meals that either Aileen or some culinary bots sifted through to find recommendations.

As I set the table, Aileen asked, "Would you like to watch TV while you eat?"

"No, thank you, Aileen."

"Do you want to listen to your new playlist."

"No, thank you, Aileen. I want to finish Libby's book."

I ate alone in silence, reading the end of my book. Aileen didn't say another word. When I poured my third glass of water, I spoke out loud to the empty room. "Aileen, can you turn up the A/C? It's too warm in here."

"The temperature is at the optimum setting for the weather outside and is in line with power usage in the area."

I sighed and put my dish in the sink. I'd wash it later. Aileen could recommend a clean house but she couldn't make me do it. Granted, she could make me uncomfortable as long as I was in the house.

Inside the house.

"Aileen," I announced. "I'm going out for a drive."

"On a school night, Robert?" Was there concern in her voice? "Shouldn't you wind down and rest."

"Yeah, well, Rosey had a new playlist she wanted me to hear…"

"That was my playlist, Robert."

"And I can put the windows down and catch a breeze. Maybe drive by that ice cream parlor…"

"You just bought ice cream, Robert. It's in the freezer."

"And who knows, I might meet someone there and make a pleasant evening out of it."

Silence. I had her there. Aileen couldn't play matchmaker, and social interaction was an aspect of healthy well-being.

"Aileen, you can shut off the A/C while I'm out to save power."

I had my hand on the door when I noticed that the background buzzing had changed pitch.

"Robert. A reevaluation shows that power usage has changed in the neighborhood over the past hour. The temperature in the living room has been lowered accordingly."

"Has it now?"

"Yes, Robert. If you choose to stay, I can play the same music you would hear in the car. I can also update your dating profile and flag the false accounts if you are interested in finding companionship."

"I know this, Aileen." I smiled and sat down on the couch. "Okay, let's do that."

I hate to admit it, but in some ways, the AI takeover wasn't so bad after all. You just had to know how to work a computer.

The Fertile Valley Scrolls

I was prepared for another dry lecture from Prof. Dombrowski about things that might have been but never were. A twenty-first century tale based on events that could have transpired millennia ago, inspired by a handful of trinkets that no one fully understood. No one save myself and a handful of others from the crash landing in a valley in what would one day be known as South America. I may be registered in this class as Sam Rivers, student of history, but back then, I was Simar'vursa, first mate of the ill-fated *Coy'llurah*.

Having witnessed human civilizations grow on this planet since their infancy, classes such as this one provide some nostalgia. But they also amuse me with how much they try to explain given how little they actually know. Very much like the blind men and the elephant.

To get an idea of what it's like, try this thought experiment. Find any item once commonplace during the Depression, and show it to a random millennial. Ask them what it might have been used for. Give them a dozen more and let them construct their own narrative. It would be a humorous exercise.

That's the sort of thing I experience with these aged professors. They are children with fanciful imaginations, creating wondrous stories with little basis in reality. It's a pity, really, that some of them have devoted their entire lives to folly.

Today, however, when the lights dimmed, my amusement faded and turned to horror. With the flick of an overhead projector, itself an antique of a bygone era, two side-by-side images were displayed for all to see. Photos of scratchings on ancient papyrus.

"I have a surprise for you today," Prof. Dombrowski announced.

Indeed, he had. And none were more surprised than I, the author of those aforementioned scratchings. It was a log of our travails on a primitive planet over 1200 light-years from home. I wrote them long, long ago in the first years after the crash. We knew we couldn't just wait for the rescue that even now has yet to arrive. With the death of our chieftain, Pat'livus, it fell upon me to lead our tribe's survival efforts. I logged our community's struggle with the dwindling supplies and our progress gathering resources, building shelter, and growing crops.

Had only those exploits been revealed by the projector, it might not have been so bad, even with the references to our race and home world. However, the pages that the professor selected to expose to the class contained some personal thoughts of a more delicate nature. To say I was devastated might not go far enough.

My face flushed. All of the ship records along with my personal journals were lost so long ago. Now that they'd been recovered, it was likely that teams of aged professors were poring over them. Pictures of stodgy old academics hovering over my old diaries, attempting to translate them line by line, filled my head. I was both embarrassed and terrified just looking at the display and reading those long-forgotten notes I'd kept for no one's eyes but my own.

On the right side of that big screen, there was a simple, hand-drawn image of second mate Ja'acucha. Beneath it, I had written of the attraction I'd started to feel as the tribe started to domesticate.

I was so stunned that I didn't feel the tap on my arm when my classmate wanted me to pass back the pile of printed copies. That's when I realized the professor was speaking.

"As I've mentioned before, I am occasionally asked to consult on ancient documents written in dead languages. The TA is passing out but two fragments of a larger, longer document found in caves in Argentina. I've spent many months helping to decipher them.

"We've started to make some progress, discovering patterns in the text. While it bears some resemblance to other proto-Incan dialects, this is something almost entirely new to us. And you are among the first to see it."

Some of the students gasped or applauded. I did neither of those things.

I *was* the first to see it! And now I could do nothing but hold my head in my hands. I stared down at the words describing my love and my longing for my old shipmate. That was before she'd sailed off across the great sea with Fra'onkln, an old friend whom I'd never considered a rival before then. That was thousands of years ago, but I still felt the sting of the old wound reopening.

Tears welled in my eyes as I listened to the lecture, waiting for my deep secrets to be laid bare.

"We know that the first image describes a great people who emigrated to the region. We are certain that they traveled a long way. Perhaps all the way from Central America, or even from the land bridge to Asia. Then there is this reference here."

He highlighted a piece of text.

"There is some debate about whether it is about a creator, or a crater, or even a cradle of life." He laughed. "The similarity of those words is coincidence. I wanted to see if you're still listening."

Were they? I didn't know. But I was listening, and waiting, and dreading.

"The second excerpt appears to be about agriculture."

About what? Agriculture? The emotional haze dimming my senses cleared immediately. Bolting upright in my seat, I sat in rapt attention as the professor continued.

"From the Incan words we recognize, we can tell that there are references to great mountains, which are obviously a reference to the Andes, and then a wonderful fertile valley. There are desires to plow the field and sow seeds and cultivate the land, Ja'acucha, in the time to come."

The young man in front of me snickered. He leaned to the girl beside him. "Do you know what that sounds like? *Plowing the fertile valley of Ja'acucha.*" He laughed some more as I winced as his perceptiveness.

The young lady had the decency to smack his arm. "Don't be rude. There were just farmers living through tough times."

Old academics, making up stories. This one missed the mark, but it hit so close to home. Our new home, that is. Farmers, were we?

Yes, I guess we were after a fashion. But we were also lovers. And nothing is tougher on a being than several thousand years of unrequited love. Even now, I wonder where their ship landed. I don't think I ever found out. Some memories fade with the passage of time. As it was, I couldn't even recall writing some of the text that appeared on the photocopied handouts even though they were penned by my hand. What else had I written on those "Fertile Valley Scrolls," I wondered.

And then I wondered if a student such as myself could get access to the copies of these scrolls. What I wouldn't give to relive those early days one evening. I'd sit by an open campfire and read them under the stars. Then I'd burn each page as I went, and watch the embers climb up to the heavens. And I'd wonder if she was looking up at the same stars as I, still watching for the rescue ship.

Growing Up on Unity Station

A Rigellian, an Eridanian, and a Terran walked into a bar. Each of us banged our heads because the bar had been set too low. None of us three, who are among the tallest in our kindergarten class, had been paying much attention to where we were going in the first place. We were having too much fun joking around. Above us, hanging from the top tiers of the monkey bars, some of the other kids, a Centauran, a Sirian, two Lalandeans and a big Barnard in particular, laughed at us. The learning facilitators ran over and brought us to med unit to have our heads examined. Rigellians bruise the easiest, while Eridanians are of pretty hearty stock. But we three boys played it up and got to skip afternoon classes for ice packs and lollipops.

That was how our friendship was formed. Nahg, Tec, and Bob, which are short for G'nahggistahk, Tecmishulla-something, and Robert. Okay, my name isn't as exotic as the others, but Nahg thinks it is. We shortened them all a bit just to make things easier to say and remember. I was five years old and had already met my best friends for life!

Each of us was a handful to deal with on our own. But together, there wasn't anyone who could take us on. By the end of Unity station's orbital year, we were the kings of the monkey bars. Even Big Barnard paid attention to us—he'd even bring us things, so we'd like him more. But we always made him give the stuff to the crying kid who he'd probably taken it from in the first place.

As we started to get older though, I noticed something odd about my pals. At school, everyone brought in treats to celebrate birthdays. I just assumed everyone was the same age as me (except for a certain big oaf who probably got left behind a couple times in pre-K). At home, birthdays were just a family thing. We rarely had friends over. It was a really big deal on my tenth birthday when Nahg came over because he was the only non-Terran at my party. Tec didn't show—his parents wouldn't allow it for some reason. But I was only a kid, so what did I know? Not much, except that I realized that I was already half a head taller than Nahg. Of course, my father was tall, and he'd always told me that I'd probably be bigger than he was.

That party was the last I saw of either of my best buddies for a long time. That was when I discovered that friends drift apart if you don't work to stay together. The problem is that you don't notice it happening while it's happening.

Not long after that birthday, we all moved on to different schools in different sectors of the station. "Different spokes for different folks" was something the grownups said. I didn't know at the time what that actually meant. We were told it had something to do with accommodating learning styles and growth or some other nonsense.

It was a weird feeling showing up at my new school and seeing only Terran students. Some of the faculty were of different species, particularly those teaching alien culture classes. I tried signing up for Rigellian to fulfill my foreign language requirement, because of Nahg. But that was so popular I couldn't get a spot. I had to settle for either Eridanian or Sirian. The funny thing was that I hadn't seen Tec in so long, I opted for Sirian before you could blink. And I'm glad I did because Ms. Opthfaan seemed very nice. She was this shade of green that was so … well, suffice it to say that teenaged me thought she was very nice.

Not that I had *those* thoughts then. Not yet. But she must've left an impression on me because I dated more Sirians than Terrans when I reached the upper grades. Of course, at the time, I'd only ever had three girlfriends, not counting a near miss with a flirtatious Centauran. As my Terran classmates used to tell me, not everyone in our rival high schools were rivals. And they kept pushing me to find some friendly ones at every mixed dance or competition. On weekends, we'd hang out at different food courts in different sectors. Despite my appetite, I was told by the other guys that we weren't there for any all-you-can-eat buffets. We were there to see the sights. I eventually caught on, and maybe that's when I started having *those* thoughts. Somehow, in just a few short weeks, the girls got an awful lot more attractive and a lot less annoying. After I finally started talking to some of them, the guys would joke that my favorite colors were, and by right ought to be, emerald and jade.

During those years, I only saw my best buds a couple of times. One time in tenth grade, we went to the cinema together. Tec and I were so much taller than Nahg that he was charged for a kid's ticket! I think he was embarrassed but it was hard to tell if he was blushing with his deep copper skin. Tec, on the other, had bulked out at the shoulders, and the ivory-colored bumps on his cerulean and cobalt forehead were starting to take form. He had a large, shaggy, mop of midnight bluish, flyaway tendrils, which he brushed down his hands whenever any girls walked by.

At this point, Tec was also more than an inch taller than me. He said he'd just endured his first growth spurt. I'd probably catch up with him at some point, especially since Eridanian average is three inches shorter than Terran.

When I'd turned eighteen and finally finished fourteen years of school, I had to prepare to enter the workforce. Mom fretted that I was already looking for my own apartment, but I think Dad was happy at the idea of having a den. My dreams were of starting a family unit of my own with the right person. I was a little saddened when I learned that Terrans and Sirians couldn't produce children together. Ms. Opthfaan, who posed with me in a graduation photo that I'll always treasure, never had reason to bring that up. However, she did cover their genetic ancestral cultural memory, which I guess would be an issue with mixed pairings.

Life was ready to pull me into a new orbit like a stray asteroid getting a gravitational tug from a larger unmovable body. But before it could force me away for good, I looked up my two oldest friends. There were no parents or principals to separate us from each other anymore.

My new place had its own terminal screen, and I used a chunk of my time and data allotments tracking them down.

I found Tec just days before he was set to move to a different station orbiting farther out from the sun. The window for commuting there opened up for only a couple weeks every two years or so. Naturally, I went down to the port to wish him safe travels. I spent half an hour looking, but I couldn't find him. While I stood there staring at the departure schedule, a blue hand settled on my shoulder. "Bob! I'm so glad you came!"

I turned and saw an older Eridanian standing next to me. Not *old*, just older than I was, and about two inches shorter. I had to squint a little before I realized that this person in front of me really was Tec. I didn't recognize him dressed in that slightly worn business suit. His horns had turned upward and grown to three inches in length. He also had lines developing down either side of his face. His tendrils were thinning more than I thought it should be. On top of all that, his voice was deeper than ever before.

"Work's been crazy the past couple years, you know." I knew they were his words, but it seemed like they were coming out of a stranger's mouth. "But there's a great opportunity on the Horizon station. Can you believe it? After only two years working with the maintenance crews, I'm up for an assistant manager position. Once I complete the training course, that is, but I'm told it'll be a cinch!"

He lifted his hands to his face and rubbed his cheeks. Then he ran them through his tendrils, brushing them back. "When I'm settled, I'll send you a message. You're out of school now, right?"

Couple years? Out of school? I had no idea what he was talking about. If we'd started school together, then he should've just graduated like I had. I wanted to know if something had caused him to drop out, but I honestly didn't know how to ask. I was still pondering this when a voice croaked out behind us.

"Hey, guys!" Turning about, I saw Nahg running up. I'd swear his voice cracked each time he spoke. His face looked like it had the Rigellian version of pimples. He was wearing a school jacket that had a Rigellian letter emblazoned on the front. Nahg grabbed Tec and gave him a hug. "Good luck, man! I bet you can't wait until you can shake the dust of this station off your boots!"

I was totally confused, but I wished Tec good luck and watched him board his shuttle. Then I looked at Nahg and asked him, "Hey, do you want to grab a pint and just catch up?"

Tec laughed too loudly for too long. "Bob, you don't get it, do you? They won't serve me anything. I'm still a minor. I'm not old enough!"

"What do you mean? Aren't you my age? How old are you?"

Nahg stopped laughing and caught his breath. He had a big grin on his face when he informed me of something that had never occurred to me. "I just turned thirty-one, in Standard years. But Rigellians don't become adults until their forty-fifth birthday."

"Wait, I don't understand. When we met, you were—"

"Eighteen. But I was a little bit of late bloomer."

I'd never learned about Rigellian lifespans, nor had I ever asked about them. Nahg was actually closer to my mom's age than to mine. Suddenly, a mental image of those lines down my Eridanian friend's face flashed before my eyes. "So how old is Tec?"

"He's seventeen now. He was four back in kindergarten. Can you imagine? He's younger now than when I was when we first met! And he's been a working stiff for two years already." Nahg grabbed my arm and pointed to an empty bench. I think he realized that I needed to sit down before he could explain things to me. So, we sat.

"Did you ever wonder why our parents didn't like us hanging around together so much? It was because of how we all age. Do you realize that by the time I'm old enough for that pint you wanted to buy me, Tec will be an old man. And that's if he makes it that long. I mean, I hope he does, but he'll be thirty-one — my age now — and that's well into Eridanian retirement. To me, well, he's not quite what a butterfly is to you, but you get the idea. We were never going to be drinking buddies unless I sneak a bottle into his senior center."

My head was spinning. How had I never realized any of this? Maybe because all the adults always seemed so old that I just I figured us kids were all the same in every way. You know, except for color, horns, vestigial tails, and the like.

I was deep in thought when I noticed Nahg tugging on my jacket, snapping me out of it. "So, Bob, while you're here, can you do me one favor?"

"Um, yeah. I guess. What is it?"

He looked around and over both shoulders. It seemed like his usual copper red face was turning a little crimson. He stuck his hands in his pockets and stared at the ground. "Well, there's going to be this party, with friends from school. There might even be a few girls there. And I was wondering..." He pulled some crumpled currency out of his pocket. "Could you buy me a couple of six-packs?"

All those years of schooling had transformed me into a responsible adult, hadn't they? But still, I wondered. Maybe not quite yet. I took the money and stuffed it into my pocket. Nahg and I have been friends for almost my entire life and more than half of his. I'd had friends who'd helped get me through some awkward times in school. This was a chance to pay it forward. It was the least I could do for a shy Rigellian entering his turbulent thirties and who was, as I would come to learn, in the early years of a decade-long bout of puberty.

I said that I would, and I asked him to find out if that party was being chaperoned by anyone's older sister. I also made a mental note to find out how genetically compatible our races are. Maybe there was a fifty-odd year old Rigellian woman willing to put up with a more quickly aging Terran male for her forty or fifty child-bearing years. Maybe emerald and jade might give way to copper and garnet.

Instead of going out for that beer, I offered to treat Nahg to the cinema. I was curious what a "teen" Rigellian romance flick was like. And I wanted to do a little research.

That Time Everything Went Haywire

IT WAS THE FIRST SUNNY MORNING AFTER NEARLY A FULL WEEK OF DREARY, rainy days. I got dressed early, which for me was about half past nine, because I wanted to make sure I spent some time outside. With keys, wallet, and phone in hand, I decided to head for the park. It might still be muddy, but I figured I could still walk a couple of laps around the lake. Then I passed the donut shop on the avenue, when it occurred to me that I could sit and enjoy the sights and sounds from a park bench while drinking an iced latte and chowing down on a cruller. Added bonus, doing this would eliminate the worry of walking into a tree while texting.

A half block later, I passed Cosmic Realities Comic Stop, by which I mean that I didn't pass it at all. It's not my fault! There's a stop sign right there in the shop name. I was just obeying the law, I told myself.

As soon as I crossed the threshold, I got a "Hey, Steve," from Ralphie, the manager, followed by "leave the latte on the front counter." That didn't bother me since I was only planning on staying for a few minutes. Just long enough to thumb through a couple of graphic novels. Somewhere around the third or fourth book, I promised myself I'd be off to the park after the next one. Or the one after that.

"As long as you're here, Steve, there's a card game demo at noon."

"Thanks, Ralph, but no. Not staying that long."

It wasn't until I'd looked over my shoulder back at the front counter that I realized that there was an in-store promotion going on this morning. I'd been facing the racks, so I hadn't noticed the table with the piles of an indie comic production behind me. After that the creator tried to get my attention each time I picked up a book from the shelves. On his fourth or fifth attempt, I gave in and walked over.

The guy had crazy hair, a computer code T-shirt, and a reputation that preceded him.

Henry Weir, and his strong opinions, were regular fixtures as Cosmic. He also trolled the digital world under the username *Haywire13*.

Wherever he was, he'd always preach the one true way to do whatever it was anyone else was doing. I didn't follow his antics, but my buddy Art would occasionally engage him using the most perfect and understated mocking tone. These counterpunches let the world know just how full of himself Weir actually was.

Now, it turned out, he was also an independent comic creator. As loathsome a presence as he was online, I had to give him props for pursuing his dream. I wasn't interested in giving this guy any money, but I thought it couldn't hurt to just take a look. Keep in mind, not a single decision I'd made so far that morning had turned out as planned.

The title of Weir's book, which came as no shock to me, was *Haywire 13*. Nor was I surprised to see that he had already produced five issues and was hawking a collected anthology to boot. Heavy on the blue tones, *Haywire* featured a morally gray antihero, named Haywire, who hunted across the dark web. And, by issue three, he could travel in time to both the far future and back to the Industrial Revolution, by computer.

Weir flipped open the issue to locate a specific panel on a particular page. "It's possible because Haywire learned the secret of the One True Method of time travel."

Uh huh. I started to state an opposing viewpoint and realized too late what a mistake that was. I'd opened the floodgate to the Weir Theory of what was and wasn't possible in temporal physics, not to mention techno-magic. For the next ten minutes, or possibly thirteen hours, I listened to a rambling dissertation. Could a person travel physically, or only ethereally? How would just one body affect everything?

Was it really a butterfly effect or was it more like a worm or a virus?

He pointed to a bright, flashy page with a lot of text bubbles. "And that proves that energy would be conserved if a stream of data, like a digital file or even just a text, were transmitted through space-time."

Quietly, I stood there listening. I wished that a message from the future would've warned me about coming into the shop today. If only such things were possible!

"And remember," he seemed to be concluding at long last. "If you weren't careful, if you made the smallest mistake, everything would go…" He paused for effect, but I knew what was coming. "…*Haywire!*"

Having only myself to blame for the poor choices I made that got me here, I tried to excuse myself during this lull. It took four more "okays" and "good days" afterward before I could break free.

Generally, I prefer my superheroes larger than life and unambiguous, the usual four-color fare. When it came to science fiction, grimdark antiheros aren't my wheelhouse. I tended toward hopeful futures, visiting worlds I'd want to live in. I've fancied myself the hero of my own imagined future-tech stories. In those, the worst that could be said is that if someone were to break some rule or to stray into the gray, it would be in the name of all things good. Keep my protagonists *Lawful* or at least *Neutral Good*, if you please.

After losing an hour and a half, I grabbed a book to buy from the shelf, mostly out of guilt and returned to the front. Ralphie rang up my purchase, which he stuck first into a plastic sleeve and then a paper bag. He slid it across the counter, leaving it next to my room-temperature latte and slightly stale donut.

Then Ralphie pointed to a box of game cards a couple inches away from my bag. The cover image had a ship's pilot at the wheel along with stars, lasers, and a half-existing space cat. "Sure you won't hang around for the demo. It starts in a few minutes."

I'd already been in here too long, wasting my beautiful day away, so I politely declined.

"Nah," I said. "It's too nice outside to be stuck indoors." I scooped up my stuff and stepped out once again into the light of day.

My timing was perfect. My buddy, Art, was walking up the street toward me.

"How's it hanging, bud?" I asked. I shifted everything into my left hand and raised my right arm, anticipating a high five.

"Doing good, Steve." A loud slap accompanied the joining of our hands, followed by a manly bro-hug that broke after three *Mississippi's*. "Hey, are you going to be around in a half hour? I got an appointment with Maria in a couple minutes."

Art pointed his thumb over his shoulder to Gino's barbershop, which was next to the comic store. Gino owned the place, but his daughter, Maria, styled hair in a way that she — and many of the other neighborhood ladies — found attractive. If you just wanted a cut, you walked in and got Gino. If you wanted to look good, you made an appointment and waited for Maria.

I glanced up at the clear sky for a minute. The sun above proclaimed that the morning was over., The day wasn't getting any younger. Then I looked back at Art, who I hadn't had a chance to hang with in a while.

"Sure thing. They're about to demo a new card game in the store. Maybe I can still grab a spot at the table."

An electronic bell announced the comic shop door opening. Crazy-haired Haywire shuffled out, holding a shipping box piled high with his product line. He stopped suddenly, and I figured that his eyes were just adjusting to the sunshine. But then I realized but they were just resting on Art.

"*You!* I knew I'd see you again!"

Weir dropped the box to the ground, spilling his inventory all over the concrete. He didn't seem to care much about his books because he launched himself at Art. I didn't know what was going on, but Art must have. He pushed me aside and out of the way.

I slipped on a stray comic and went down on my hands and knees. The fall to the pavement splattered my drink and crushed my cruller. I also might've sprained my wrist and bumped my head while this was going on. It happened so quickly I don't remember.

When I looked up, I saw that Art had leaned a little to his right and deflected Weir, who careened into a parked Camry. He hit it hard enough to leave a dent and set off the alarm. Weir swung around, fists up. Art crouched, ready for action.

My head swam more than all the water-based superheroes whose names I couldn't remember just then. I tried to scramble to my feet but found that I couldn't. And right there, in that instant of me trying to gain my footing and intercede in a fight, my phone trilled. What cosmic force is it that has trained us so that even in the direst of circumstances, we have to glance down at that tweet or IM or whatever, rather than face the immediate crisis in front of us? I don't know. But despite the chaos ensuing about me, I stopped to read the text.

It said: "*Whatever you do, don't interfere.*"

The crazy part: the text was from *me*. From my own phone number.

How? I didn't know. But I'd sent it. Between the bump on my head and this, I couldn't think or move. I just sat back on my ankles for the next moment or two.

By then, it was too late to get between the two of them. They had gone from throwing punches to wrestling each other on the sidewalk. They tumbled over, back, and forth, each claiming the upper hand, only to lose it again a moment later. By this point, some of the guys came out of the shop. Now that we had an audience, I knew I'd have to help break it up. Otherwise, I'd look like a coward who didn't help his friend.

As I took a step up, a shot rang out. I immediately dropped back down to the cement again. Everyone else froze in place, including the two combatants.

A second shot sounded, and Gino's front window shattered. Alarms screeched. The gunman ran out onto the sidewalk. He stopped dead in his tracks when he saw all of us. After a quick count of the number of spectators that had eyes on him, he turned and fled in the other direction.

Police sirens started blaring. Art was the first to reclaim his wits. He lifted himself up to one knee. Then he shook Weir's shoulder and offered him a hand up. "Hey, we, uh, need to talk. What's say we go grab some coffee after we're done with the cops."

Weir hesitated a moment but accepted the help. He was a little shaky on his feet. After he took a few deep breaths, he nodded and muttered a quiet, "Okay, man. Yeah."

I stood as still as a statue in a hall of justice as cops arrived on the scene. I looked at my phone again. "Don't interfere," it still read. That hadn't changed, not that I'd expected it to. The crazy, unexplained warning that I'd sent myself hadn't self-destructed in five seconds. Staring at it got me thinking.

Had Weir's confrontation saved Art's life? Would he have taken a bullet had he walked into the barbershop? Would I have gotten Art killed had I stopped the fight? And how did I—or how will I—send that text? Did I actually send a stream of data through time?

Having laid low and done nothing today, would I one day be the hero of this story?

It was all too confusing. I didn't want to think about it. Or anything else, for that matter. Not the shooting, not the implications for the future. Had I just altered it? Would I become some kind of chrono-wizard?

No more thinking. I just wanted to go back inside and play a mindless demo with imaginary space lasers after the police questioned me about the all-too-real bullets.

I looked up at the yellow ball in the sky and decided that the sunshine could wait another hour. I still had the afternoon.

Last Dance, Last Chance

It was near closing at the Well, a quiet dive for less discriminating folks low on cash. Just a handful of us remained. The college crowd had come for a peaceful round or two away from loud music before they move on to a diner or a backseat somewhere. Some of the girls, with their ears obviously still ringing, are blathering about the rest of the Well's clientele louder than they realize.

But that's okay. I'm over college girls anyway.

The brunette at the bar was more my speed. She wasn't quite young enough to pull off her miniskirt, not that I had a problem with it. But on top, she looked like cotton candy in a cashmere sweater of candy-floss pink. It reminded me of the color of my college girlfriend's cheeks on cool autumn nights.

This woman's face was pale with some rogue blended in. It was a face that once held the promise of the stars and now held the reality of the streets. It was something I could relate to.

I stepped over to the bar, introduced myself as Joey, and offered to buy a drink. She accepted and then humored my attempts at a conversation. Mostly, she kept her eyes on the bar in front of her. The lady was guarded, offering up very little information about herself. I didn't even get a name. A chance comment clued me in that she worked in a classroom. When I'd asked what she could teach me, she said that she could definitely teach me a thing or two.

I wasn't sure how to take that, or even what to say next. When the jukebox started playing an old ballad, she cocked her head to one side and brushed her hair back. I wondered if it had been her quarter that selected it. I closed my eyes and listened for a moment. When I opened them again, I had the nerve to ask, "Can you teach me how to dance real slow?"

It was a cheesy line, sure. But it got her to look up at me. Those bright red lips on her powdered face gave me a wry smile. She appeared to be considering my semi-decent proposal. It was the best shot my self-esteem had had all night, and it hadn't come from a bottle. More than just my marks were rising. My back straightened, my shoulders went back and my chin lifted. I might've shown a hint of a slight, satisfied smile.

"Why not?" she purred. She slid down from her stool, and had no trouble sticking the landing in her three-inch heels. As she tugged the hem of her skirt and adjusted her sweater, I noticed that she stood nearly a full foot shorter than me, although her hair made up for several inches. The lady downed the rest of her free drink in one gulp and set the empty mug on the bar. "You can't be too careful leaving a drink about."

"No, you can't be, uh…"

"You can call me Dolores."

"No, you can't be too careful, Dolores."

I swallowed the last couple mouthfuls of my beer, nearly spilling some out of my mouth in the process. I wasn't worried my drink might get spiked — more that it might get swept off with the empties. I'd hate to waste good beer... or even this stuff.

Dolores took charge, and I followed her instructions willingly. She took my hand and glided out to the middle of the room. Then she turned toward me and placed both my hands on her hips. "These go here," she said, teacher voice engaged. Then she cautioned me more sternly, "and *only* here."

I was a little woozy from downing that last pint, not to mention the ones before it, but I didn't complain.

Without warning, she put her arms around me and pulled me in closer. That pink sweater pressed up against me. But given the height difference, it wasn't the small of my back she grabbed. I didn't complain about that, either. To be fair, I never told her where my "here" was.

A few beats later, her hands were on my arms, and her cheek was pressed against my chest. For a moment, I was back at college.

"Just sway your hips to the music," she said.

The music? I was barely aware of it anymore. But my hips swayed in concert with hers. My body leaned in, and I thought maybe the world was spinning a little slower. I grinned at our reflection in the bar mirror. But my little smirk faded when I glimpsed the clock over the register. The world still spun as it always had, and clocks moved at their regular pace. Closing time was coming too soon. Or maybe, I thought, not soon enough?

When the song ended, Dolores gently pushed away. She looked up at me with smiling, but sad eyes. "I'll be right back. I'm going to freshen up." I watched her walk away. My only two thoughts were how much I liked her in that sweater, and how much I wanted to see her out of it. You can probably guess which thought was winning as she passed through the dim lights and disappeared into the dark hallway leading to the rest rooms in the back.

I returned to my barstool for a final round. Last call was upon us, and I ordered one more beer for the road.

"And the lady?" the bartender asked.

I looked down at her empty glass next to me. "Wait until she gets back."

A full glass on the bar might make her suspicious when she returned.

The minute hand on the bar's clock inched closer to twelve. I began to wonder if she was going to return from the ladies' room at all. By closing time, I figured out that she'd used the back door. I was going home alone.

Dolores, if that had actually been her name, had left a couple dollars on the bar. But she'd taken her purse with her. She'd also taken was my wallet, boosting it when she grabbed my ass.

Not a great loss. The wallet, I mean. After a few hours of drinking, my cheap, imitation leather wallet was empty. All the money I had left on me was on the counter in front of my glass. There was still enough for me to leave a tip and pay for a ride home. But, of course, I ordered a last shot of rye. That left me walking.

Getting a new wallet was really no big deal. And one phone call would cancel my bank card. On the other hand, replacing my ID meant a trip down to DMV. That was going to be a bigger pain than one little whiskey would soothe.

But still, I raised the glass and toasted Dolores because for just a few moments, she'd brought me back down to a happier time. And honestly, the dance was totally worth it.

Taking the World by Storm!

Blair sat on the last stool in the corner at the window counter of *Talk Wordy to Me*, a trendy bookshop café, engrossed in a novel. She was oblivious to the masses of pedestrians on the crowded sidewalk outside scurrying past with their umbrellas braced against the wind and the driving rain. Her once-steaming coffee sat neglected as she turned page after page to the point that she no longer paid her coffee any mind. Nor did she give much attention to the stranger who sat down next to her. Until he dared to speak to her.

"Hey, that's that book."

The intruding voice took her out of the moment. She looked over and saw a gentleman smiling at her. Mid-30s, perhaps, but definitely five to ten years her senior, and wearing a dark suit and red tie under an overcoat soaked by the rain. She glanced behind him to see that all the seats at the counter were occupied, so he probably hadn't singled her out when he sat. But that also meant that there were no other seats that she could retreat to, either. Too many people had come into the store, taking shelter from the storm outside.

"That's the book everyone's talking about," he tried again. "About the great storm that's coming."

She decided she would politely, but briefly, engage the man with the intent of ending the conversation before it went too far. Blair closed the book with her index finger holding her place and showed the stranger the title on the cover of "that book."

"Yes, it's *Taking the World by Storm*. And, yes, everyone's reading it. It's new. It's a bestseller. And they have a dozen copies for sale on the rack over there if you'd like one." Blair turned away before a storm of her own started forming. She reopened the book and put her nose close to it to hide her face. Believing her point had been made, she then pulled it away a little so her eyes could focus on the page.

Unfortunately, the gentleman hadn't taken the hint.

"Excuse me, but I was on my way to an interview. I just stepped in here to get out of the rain for a minute. I couldn't help but notice how many people are reading that book. So I guess it really is 'taking the world by storm.'" The man laughing at his own obvious joke made Blair cringe inside a little. Then he asked, "Are you enjoying it? Do you think it's any good?"

A puff of air escaped her lips, launching some stray hairs toward the ceiling. Blair closed the book again with her finger still in place. Next, she removed her glasses with her other hand and placed them on the counter next to her cup so she could rub her eyes. "Look, if it wasn't good, would so many people be reading it?"

"I'm sorry," he said. It seemed like he'd started to realize that he was intruding. "But you never know what will make people buy a book and make it a bestseller, let alone such a viral success. I'm trying to understand why. What is it that everyone likes about it? Why does it resonate with folks so much?"

"I can't speak for 'folks.' But it speaks to me. It speaks to anyone who's suffered adversity in the face of an oncoming storm. It speaks to anyone who's ever been in a stormy relationship. It speaks to women. Maybe that's something you could learn from the book."

"Believe me…" The gentlemen stared out the window at the people scurrying about driving rain. "I've been trying to learn. But I'm just left with more questions. I know it's a good book, but the response has been overwhelming. Do you think it's possible that some readers may be reading more into it? Putting their own experiences into the text? What I mean is, is it possible that some of the fans are finding meanings in the book that weren't intended or aren't there?"

Blair picked up her coffee and took a sip. She winced when she realized how cold it had gotten. So she took out her displeasure on the stranger. "Well, if reading the book didn't help you, I don't know that I can. Maybe you can interview more people. A lot more, different, other people. There are plenty around."

"Okay, okay. I can take a hint," he protested.

She shot him a look because that was obviously not true. She'd stopped dropping hints back while her coffee was still warm. "And why don't you do the ladies here a favor and ask some of the men."

"If I find some men who've read it, I'll do just that. Thank you. And have a good day, Miss ..." After an awkward gap, he stood. "My name's Paul, by the way. It was nice talking with you."

"Have a good day," she said, not repeating his name, nor even raising her eyes. Blair listened as Paul's footsteps receded. She didn't care if he'd found another seat in the café or if he'd stepped back out into the rain. *Just go bother someone else,* she thought. *Or go to your interview and annoy them.*

Blair put her coffee down and reached for a napkin. But in doing so she knocked over her cup, spilling it everywhere. She jumped up quickly before any could get drip on her clothes. "Idiot!" she cursed quietly. In her mind, she was blaming the stranger for her own carelessness. She found a dry spot to put the book and grabbed some more napkins to contain the spill.

When the mess had been cleaned up, the cup and napkins disposed of, and her hands sanitized, Blair went to retrieve her hardcover. She stopped and stared when she noticed the photograph on the book's back cover. Looking up at her was a picture of Paul King, the author, a smiling mid-30s gentleman who had just recently taken the world by storm.

You May Now
Fight the Bride

BERNIE STOOD ON THE OUTDOOR ALTAR BEFORE THE PARSON AND NEXT TO his beautiful bride. He gazed upon Morrigan's lovely visage and thought himself the luckiest man alive. Watching how her green eyes sparkled was like seeing the sun dance across the morning dew in a field of ivy. Her fiery red hair was braided in an elaborate knot. And she was crowned with a wreath of wildflowers and holly.

He still couldn't believe the summer they'd had, the whirlwind romance. In such a short time, he knew he wanted to be with her forever. He was ready to leave big-city life behind and move up north to a small, quiet town for the rest of his days.

And now they were here, exchanging rings and reciting vows in the little garden, surrounded by trees, flowers, and two dozen folding chairs. Morrigan's family, her "clan" as she liked to call them, comprised most of the small crowd that gathered to witness the nuptials.

He wouldn't have wanted this moment to end, except that he couldn't wait for the next moment to begin, and each moment after, for as long as they both should live.

Through his euphoria, Bernie heard the parson say, "Morrigan and Bernard, you have stated your intentions. You have spoken your hearts and made your promises to each other. Bernard, you may now fight the bride."

Bernie leaned in to kiss his love and stopped suddenly. She had already taken a step away from him. The flower girl and the ring bearer had come down the nave, each carrying a large satin pillow with a sword resting atop it. Morrigan snatched one and hefted the weapon high to feel its weight.

"Wait! What?"

Bernie couldn't have been more puzzled by a London crossword with half the clue smeared by rain. Or tears.

The parson replied, "As is the custom of the ancient warrior clans, you must win her love. In battle."

"In battle? With the woman I just married? I thought I'd already won her love!"

The flat of his bride's blade struck Bernie across the seat of his pants.

"Defend yourself!" Morrigan cried out, before retreating two steps and readying her bastard sword once more.

"Technically," the parson interjected, "you are not yet married. And you've only defeated the other suitors."

Bernie looked to his almost-wife and back to parson. "I've never struck a woman in my life! I'm not about to start now."

With a growl, Morrigan crouched, preparing for her next assault.

The parson said, "You may find it difficult striking this one now as well. However, it should be enough to disarm her." The holy man waved an arm to the ring bearer. The bastard sword he bore had "Bernard" engraved on the blade.

"Of course," the parson continued, "if you feel unable, you could have your second fight for you."

Realizing what that meant, Quentin, Bernie's little brother and best man, took a step back.

"However, should he win, he would earn the right of the first night."

Before Quentin could step forward again, his two older brothers held him in place, just in case.

"FIGHT ME, YOU MANGY CUR!"

There was another growl, and Morrigan launched herself at the man who would win her heart. Bernie grabbed the handle of the sword and managed to lift just in time. He blocked a swing coming at his head. The force of the blow shook his entire body and sent him stumbling several paces to his right.

"YE WOULD HAVE ME?" Morrigan threw her arms wide. "THEN CLAIM ME!" She crouched low, seeking to sweep Bernie's legs.

Somehow, Bernie managed to jump over the blade, which nearly nicked his soles as it passed beneath. Morrigan was thrown off-balance for a moment. She quickly recovered and reversed her attack.

Focusing solely on the sword swinging at him, Bernie jumped and came down on the blade. He forced it to the ground. Morrigan stumbled forward on her hands and knees. Disarmed and helpless, she raised her head in defeat, with eyes pleading.

Bernie took a deep breath and shook his head. Dropping his sword to the grass, he took a step toward his bride and extended his hand.

Morrigan pulled herself up... and threw a left hook into Bernie's face. The groom staggered back.

"I thought you said I just had to disarm her!"

"You didn't force her to yield."

Morrigan charged the man who would be her husband. Her raised right hand was adorned with sharply manicured nails. Bernie threw his arms wide open. At the last moment, he lunged forward and executed a bear hug that pinned both of Morrigan's arms to her side and pressed her to his chest. Her warrior spirit thrashed from side to side. Bernie had the advantage of an extra eight inches in height and nearly a hundred pounds.

The woman growled, cursed, and spat before finally settling into Bernie's arms. A pouty face looked up into his eyes. From experience, Bernie knew to *never* trust that face. He relaxed his arms for a fraction of a second and then squeezed them tighter than before.

Morrigan fought to breathe. She managed to place her hands on Bernie's hips. Then she said, "Bernard... I yield... my love... to you."

The groom turned his head to the parson, who nodded his assent. At last, Bernie could release the breath he hadn't realized that he'd been holding.

His almost-wife smiled at him when he relaxed his arms. He leaned down for a long, deep first kiss, which was eagerly received and reciprocated. Bernie placed one hand upon his wife's back with the other supporting the back of her head.

Morrigan slid her hands up from her husband's hips. Then she hooked her thumbs into the adjustable elastic at the rented tux's waist. In one quick maneuver, she yanked Bernie slacks down to his knees, revealing his red satin, heart-covered boxers.

"But..." Morrigan declared defiantly, "I claim the pants in the marriage."

My Mother, the GPS

THANKS TO A SWARM OF IDIOT DRIVERS, I HAD TURNED OFF THE INTERSTATE and driven onto a winding back road. It wasn't exactly a shortcut, but it was soothing to my nerves. I figured that having the road to myself might save me some time anyway. However, despite being alone in the car, I still heard a loud complaint about my route change being voiced. *"Recalculating!"*

She always sounded so annoyed with me.

"Recalculating!" she repeated. It was the same tone, and yet she seemed even angrier. She settled down and gave me a few peaceful moments.

When I approached a jug handle where I could circle back to my original route, that was her cue. She spoke up once again. *"In 100 yards, make a right."*

I had no intention of turning back. That would be admitting defeat or making a mistake. So I blew past the turnoff.

"Recalculating!"

This time, the voice was definitely different. It wasn't annoyed. Did she just sigh at me? Could a GPS be disappointed?

"You never listen to me," she said.*" I'm only thinking of what's best for you…"*

I glanced at the dash long enough that I nearly clipped a tree that was edging its way into the side of the road at the next bend. "Mom?"

"I could talk to you until I was blue in the face…"

"Ma, is that you in there?"

"But you always had to do what you wanted. You had to do it your way. And where did it get you now? I'm just your GPS, and even I'm not sure!"

"Ma-ah!"

"Yes, sweetheart."

Checking the road, I swerved around a dead squirrel, and ran over a fallen branch. I kept checking my mirrors for signs of any other vehicles. And I glanced at all the vents to see if any kind of smoke or fumes was escaping. Nothing. I wasn't hallucinating.

This had to be a gag. A programming trick by one of my envious siblings. Jealous because Mom always liked me best.

"Mom, how are you in my GPS?"

"I don't know, dear. I was just on a cloud talking with your Aunt Marie..."

"Aunt Marie? She's been gone since I was, like, five!"

"Yes, and it's been wonderful catching up. Now don't interrupt. I taught you better than that. Anyway, we were talking, and I guess I was saying... I think you want to make a left up here, dear... I was saying to Aunt Marie how much I missed my little Kevvy-wevvins."

"Ma-a-a-a! I'm twenty-six! Please stop calling me that."

"Fine. Talk to your mother that way. You'll miss this when you're forty."

I looked back at the road. We were, I mean *I was*, coming to a fork. The left road would take me down and around the lake. That actually might be quicker, and more calming, too. That is, if I wasn't dealing with...

"At the fork, bear left."

Right, Mom. I turned left.

As the trees rose up on the road behind me, the ones in front of me parted and yielded a serene lake view. In a moment of tranquility, I found my voice again. "So you're here. Now what? Are you staying in my car?"

There was silence as I pulled onto Lake Road. There was a sleepy little hamlet coming up. Past that, I could swing around to state road 15, which would cut across back to the interstate. I wondered if the GPS would go back to normal then if I returned to the original route I'd planned out.

"Stop the car," she told me. *"In 400 yards, turn left, and park at the shore."*

"What?"

"We never had a chance to just sit down and have a good mother-son chat. There are things I need to tell you. There are things you should know."

This was just too crazy. It has to be my sister and brother playing a joke on me. Probably it was Tricia's idea, with Richie doing the technical stuff. Either way, though. I pulled over and shut off the car. I fumbled for my phone, trying to decide which of them I'd call first to give an earful about this.

"Is the lake pretty, Kevv — Is it pretty, Kevin? It looks nice on the map. Is it pretty to look at?"

"Yes, Mom. It is. I never really stopped to notice it before. I usually speed past lakes." I watched some Canadian geese paddle about for a moment. "So, what did you want to talk about?"

"So, dear, about your father... do you remember that time when he went away 'on business' for three months...?"

I didn't know where this was going. In fact, I'd totally forgotten where it was that I'd been going. And I wasn't even sure where I *wanted* to go any more. Except home, maybe. I started thinking that I just wanted to go home again.

The GPS has a button for Home.

But for the moment, it probably had a lot more stories to tell for the ride.

A Burning, Orange Flame

I ALWAYS HAVE A LOT ON MY MIND, BUT YOU WOULD NEVER KNOW IT FROM looking at me. At least, that's what people tell me. Hell, I wouldn't even know it if I went by what I saw in the mirror in the morning. The weight of the world's problems doesn't weigh down on my shoulders. It slides off my back along with any other things that don't concern me. Sometimes it occurs to me that in the big blueprint of life, I'm just such a small, redundant cog in a giant machine. I could never affect much of anything even if I wanted to. That's one of the things I think about a lot, but it doesn't really faze me much. Because nothing fazes me.

What am I supposed to do about it?

I just keep moving. No matter what happens, I keep doing what I'm doing. Just keep surviving.

It drives my girlfriend Lanie crazy sometimes, but she sticks by me. I tell myself, *Rick, you're a lucky man. Don't forget that.* She's my rock, my strength when she's with me.

But at this particular moment, I was walking alone, and focused only on what was in front of me. Shops passed by on either side of the street, but I rarely take notice of any of their displays. If I were hungry, I might think to look for a slice of pizza. If I had a headache, I'm pretty sure there's a drug store around here somewhere. Otherwise, I go from point A to point B with blinders on, oblivious to distractions. I may hear a lot of sirens as I'm moving about, but it doesn't occur to me to inquire if they're police, fire, ambulances, or whatever. I guess I could tell by the sound if I paid enough attention. But I figure if I'm still walking, they aren't coming for me, so they gain none of my interest. It's gotten to the point where I've sometimes wondered what it would actually take to distract me out of my funk.

Today, I found out.

I reached the end of Willoughby Street where the intersection comes to a T, with Livingston Park on the other side of St. Marks Avenue. Plenty of people were there doing park things: lying on the grass, sitting on the benches, feeding the birds. I've never really noticed anything in particular, even when they biked, skated, or strolled right by me. I'm only there because walking straight across the park is the quickest route to Point B.

But whatever it is that park folks normally do, I started to realize that today they weren't doing it.

Normal would be people walking about with their partners or their pets. Why were people standing still and gawking at the sky? Even I was aware that something was off. It wasn't 4:20, and the air didn't smell funky, but folks were acting strangely. Finally, curiosity got the better of me, and I looked up myself. I stopped and stood frozen like the rest of them. I just stared with my mouth agape.

There was a woman in an orange leotard flying in the air overhead with a small, steady stream of fire trailing behind her. That part actually isn't so unusual. You have to understand, that in this town, that's almost as common as seeing a squirrel stealing a nut. I'd even seen this hero in the papers. They'd called her the Orange Flame. I'd never encountered her in person before.

No, the curious thing was the man wearing the black suit dueling with her from the confines of his flying armchair. It looked comfortable with foot and head rests. Plus it had two kinds of wings, the ones you expected to see on a wingback chair and the kind you'd usually see on an airplane. On top of that, his entire contraption was encircled by a glowing ball of energy.

My first thought was if they had those in the *Williams-Sonoma* catalogue. It would beat walking. But then for some reason I couldn't explain, I started to think beyond myself and observe the conflict, which I didn't have any particular stake in.

The heroine above was throwing heat with the speed and accuracy of a major-league baller. She hurled them rapid-fire like one of those pitching machines in the batting cages, one that had been cranked up to insanity. The man remained composed. He wasted no effort swatting the ferocious balls of fire away as they simply bounced off the chair's electric aura. Thankfully, the flames snuffed themselves out before they could fall to the crowded park below.

The villain swiveled about, pitching his chair upward. The Orange Flame was doing spirals to evade something I couldn't see. I found her aerial acrobatics impressive, and you already know I'm not easily impressed. Never have been that I can remember. However, there was something about her that connected with my brain. The synapses couldn't yet construct a path from memory A to memory B but I tried to fill in the blanks.

She had skill and confidence. She exuded strength. There was this energy about her that couldn't be explained by just her burning aura. I'd never encountered a woman like that before. Not even Lanie. And let me tell you, Lanie is head and shoulders above the rest of the milling crowd. She gets me.

As I watched the battle unfold above me, I wondered if Orange Flame would get her man? Not like that. You know what I mean.

The battle had raged on for a bit when I noticed that the flying chair started to glow a different color. It propelled itself upward and flew across the Sun before swinging back around. The energy bubble fizzled away a moment right before it fired an energy blast. I could feel its energy down here on the grass. Despite the skill and grace she'd displayed earlier, the woman chose not to evade. Instead, she took the hit squarely in her stomach.

A collective gasp sounded from the crowd below her. That's when I realized how selfless this mystery hero was. Had she not flown into that energy beam, there would have been dozens of casualties on the ground. I thought back to the ambulances I'd heard speeding by earlier. Had there already been casualties?

When I looked up again, I saw that our heroine had had her fire extinguished. It also seemed that she'd lost her ability to stay aloft. She started tumbling to earth. Mid-fall, Orange Flame tried to reignite. That little burst might've been just enough to save her life, but it didn't stop her from colliding into the statue of Col. Livingston, the park's namesake. The two of them toppled to the pavement. As she lay motionless on the ground, her costume still smoldering, the flying-chair man closed in for another shot.

Something clicked inside my head at that moment. Those redundant cogs turned at a faster pace, and the fog in my brain lifted. My legs carried me forward with a burst of speed I hadn't experienced in many years. While others ran away from the danger, I ran into the heart of it. That's just what she had done when she'd flown into that first blast.

I could see she was still breathing, but her exposed midsection rose and fell with a broken rhythm. Something in my brain told me, ordered me, to take off my jacket and place it over her. Then I just stayed there, kneeling over her, shutting out the world once more, oblivious to everything else. That much was the norm for me. Anything that wasn't right in front of me could wait for my attention.

The Flame's eyes fluttered opened. Her head rolled side to side. She looked up, and locked eyes with mine. The portion of her beautiful face not obscured by her mask shrank away in horror. "No! Go… Move away…"

"No." I replied. "Let me help you the way you help others. If something happens to me—" I paused, thinking how to say it. "Tell Lanie I love her."

A powerful blast pounded my back, bringing with it a pain I'd never imagined. Not that I ever imagine pain, or even feel much of it. But this, I felt. I heard a scream, but it wasn't mine. When the blast ceased, I was holding the front of my shirt in my hands. The back had been burned away.

But I was still there. And all at once, I felt one more thing.

I felt angry.

I reached down and grabbed the foot of the fallen statue. Standing up and twisting at the waist, I flung the granite man into the sky before another shot could be fired. The direct hit sent the man on a two-second tumble to the ground. I don't know if the fall killed him or not, but I knew he wasn't walking away. That's assuming he could walk in the first place. Without its pilot, the comfy chair spiraled down and crashed into a clump of trees.

With that danger resolved, I turned my attention back to where it belonged. I felt a fire burning, not from any injury, but in my heart. I'd only ever felt a small flame kindling on a few special occasions. Now it blazed within me like a bonfire.

Orange Flame tried to sit up, and I offered her a hand. She had difficulty speaking to me. "Th-thank you… citizen. Um… that was a-ama—"

I put a finger to her lips. "Lanie, please stop."

Her eyes widened, calculating whether to admit or deny it. She didn't seem to know what to say, which was very unlike her. Lanie always knows what to say. But she also knows when to say nothing.

Besides, the proof was right in front of me.

I reached for my jacket, and she offered it willingly. I pointed to the gaping hole in her costume. At first, she moved to cover herself. Seriously? Modesty? With this much spandex?

I pointed again at the orange tulip tattoo, which looked a little like the fire I felt. "You once told me that it signifies true love."

She gasped when she saw it exposed. "Rick, I – I –"

I sat on the grass beside her and slid my arm around her back. "I get it now. I do."

Lanie leaned in with her head on my shoulder and hugged me tight. "Rick, how did you take that blast? How long have you been like this? Like an armored tank?"

"I don't know. There are a lot of things about myself that I don't know. Maybe we can figure it out together."

We sat on the grass for a while, and watched the people running about, and listened to the sirens approaching. We smelled the grass and the wildflowers and the burning wreckage. We tasted each other's lips. We felt each other's warm embrace.

And we sensed that everything would start to get better now.

Hero Crush

It started innocently enough last July. I remember that it was the fifteenth. That was the day we'd almost met. The moment I saw her, I knew that I needed to see her again. We could have a wonderful future together.

The love of my life first appeared in the skies over our city of Glens Hills about two months earlier. It was the middle of the afternoon, around the time the kids got out of school. I'd heard about her on the news, of course. They'd called her Sapphire. Oh, and what a gem she was!

One evening in June, I'd caught the barest glimpse of her in the western sky as she flew across the setting sun. But it wasn't until I was downtown on that humid July afternoon that I actually met her. Almost met her, I mean. You know, I was there, she was there. The woman who'd fallen from the terrace cafe and who'd been caught safely was there.

We were all in close proximity.

Sapphire was a wonder to behold. Statuesque, with sun-kissed skin, and short, black, curly locks. Her super outfit consisted of a deep blue, off-the-shoulder, one-piece suit that looked like something from the swimsuit issue of a padded body armor catalogue. Completing her look, she wore a yellow cape, which was attached to a chain and fastened with a gold clasp. Her accoutrement included a pair of metal bracelets, a matching stabilizer flight belt, and what looked like boots of iron.

I wondered what gear helped her to fly, or if she flew without any aid at all. She seemed to be very strong, too, to catch that woman as she did.

Before she left, Sapphire scanned the crowd. And for the briefest instant, her deep blue eyes locked with mine. In that moment, we gazed into each other's souls. I knew I was in love. She could crush my heart in her bare hands.

I left out a sigh.

And then, she was gone.

Looking up from the middle of that intersection, I watched her rise into the sky, cape fluttering behind her. And there I would've stayed in awed, reverent silence had a hand not yanked me out of the street. I heard the screech of brakes before I blacked out. I think I hit my head on the sidewalk.

"Hey, fella!" A construction worker shook me a couple of times as I opened my eyes. "You okay? You can't stand in the street like that."

Behind him, a cab driver hollered something similar, but a lot less politely. I ignored them both. All I could think of was meeting her again and coming up with a plan to make it happen.

The obvious place to start was hanging out downtown every day. The terrace cafe offered a wonderful view of the sky and a delightful menu. That meant that not only I could wave to Sapphire when I saw her, but I could also invite her to a scrumptious lunch. But she never flew by, and the daily outings were taking a bite out of my wallet.

One afternoon, out of desperation, I decided that I would jump to the street. I knew that she would swoop in and rescue me. However, when I tried to climb the café's new, reinforced railing, the waiters chased me out.

My plan had almost worked though. When I got outside, I heard her flying overhead. She could've saved me after all. Dumb waiters!

Thinking quickly, I ran into the street in front of a southbound bus. I could hear her in the wind. I also heard a policeman whistling me out of traffic. Damn. I slinked back to the curb.

The next day, I read the headline in the paper: *Sapphire Foils West-Side Robbery.*

Of course! It should have been obvious. Sapphire doesn't just save people. She fights crime, too. That's how I could meet her. Commit a crime! Nothing big, of course. I wasn't looking for real trouble. I just wanted to get her attention.

By September, I embarked on a one-man crime spree! I tried to steal an old woman's purse at the bus stop, but two other ladies beat me with theirs. I attempted to pick a pocket, but some businessmen chased after me. I saw a baby stroller in the park, and the mother on the bench was so engrossed by her phone that she was giving her child scant attention... but I'm not that kind of monster.

Frustrated, I even walked out of the diner without paying for breakfast, but I turned back, dejected, when the waitress hollered after me. I felt bad and tipped her double.

I needed to find a new approach. So I hunkered down, secluded myself, and gathered intel from newspaper stories, Internet reports, and social media videos. I studied her moves, learned her strengths, and could predict her actions. I spent most of the fall building a lab in my basement where I could work on my plan and build my confidence. It paid off in multiple ways. For one thing, I found it much easier to rob stores and commit crimes when I wasn't looking to get caught. And this got me the money I needed to continue my preparations.

In November, I drove over to Oakwood for some parts. Once there, I had an encounter with their brash new hero who called himself Magnet Man or something like that. He suffered a setback as the thrill of disarming me distracted him long enough for me to knock him down and take him out. I left him alive, but I took all his magnets and his suit. That seriously boosted my research and might have swelled my head a little. I couldn't wait to get the parts back to the lab and move up my timetable.

By the first week of January, I had moved into a warehouse on the outskirts of town.

I was finally ready to unleash my plot in February. It was the 14th, and gentlemen were rushing about getting flowers and chocolate for their ladies. Me? I subdued the drivers of an armored car for my lady love. Then I drove it to my lair for her to find. I didn't have to wait long before she was knocking on my door. Pounding through it, actually.

When she entered, I was sitting at a table for two. The candles were lit, and a bottle of champagne was on ice. "Welcome, Sapphire! I'm so glad you could make it! Join me, please."

Oddly, she seemed furious with me. She was not appreciative of the lengths to which I'd gone the past seven months just to get her attention.

"I'll join my fists to either side of your head," my lady exclaimed as she marched angrily toward me.

Sigh. I had to initiate Plan B. I pressed the button on the remote next to me, and Sapphire stopped in her tracks. The magnets beneath the warehouse floor held her boots firmly in place leaving her unable to take a step. Her fists were being pulled downward thanks to those metal bracelets. And her suit...

Uh-oh. It hadn't occurred to me that her Kevlar super suit might have been reinforced with an interwoven corset made of iron or steel! Whatever the metallic source, the magnet was tugging and yanking it downward.

"Beg your pardon!" I yelled. With eyes cast toward my feet, I scurried across the floor. No peeking, mind you. They say that the hero always peeks, but I wasn't a hero today. And, really, what kind of hero is a peeping tom?

I reached out for her cape and swung it around to the front to preserve her modesty. Now wasn't the time or the place for wardrobe malfunctions or undressing each other! Soon maybe, but not here. "I'm sorry. This isn't how I envisioned our first meeting. I wanted it to be something special."

She tested each boot again and tried to lift her hands. Then she looked right at me with those beautiful eyes and spoke only to me with those luscious lips. "Are you always this creepy with women?"

Creepy?

Sapphire wiggled beneath her cape. "Can you at least allow me to adjust myself? This isn't very comfortable."

"Oh. Certainly. Yes! Yes! Anything for you, my love!"

I think she may have winced while I ran back to the table. I grabbed the remote and dialed back the magnet's strength. I could see her raise her arms underneath the privacy of her cape. I wasn't really peeking, but I did notice that there was a bit of wiggling before I turned my head away. I was debating how I could serve the first course to her when I heard metal clanging onto the floor.

A toss of her cape revealed a stunning, statuesque pose. She was as marvelous a sight to behold as was ever beheld before. Drawn in by the vision of her beautiful face as I was, I hadn't immediately noticed that Sapphire had stepped out of her boots or that she'd flung her bracelets to the floor. That was the clanging I'd heard.

She paused for just one moment, but my mind savored it. Then this feast for the eyes hurried to join me for a feast at my table. Being the gentleman that I am, I held out a chair for her.

But instead of taking a seat, she swung her bare foot around and swept my legs. I think this might have been followed by a fist to my head because I don't recall actually hitting the floor. I only remember discovering that her strength came from neither her boots nor her bracelets. Simply put, my new girlfriend was just a whole lotta woman!

When I came around a little while later, I was sitting in the back of one of the many, many patrol cars surrounding my lair. I smiled the most satisfied, face-splitting smile to the officers up front. "Hey," I shouted, only then becoming aware of the splitting headache. "Do you wanna hear about my great first date? I'm already planning our second."

A good villain has contingencies in place. Plans had been set in motion. Wheels were already turning. I'll be ready to see her again sometime in May or possibly June. But definitely in time for our anniversary!

Family Night on Neutral Ground

Leonardo Pisano's Pizza Parlor, which many consider to have the best slices in all the West End, was neutral territory. Everyone wanted to enjoy their tomato sauce and that cheesy goodness. Or wallow in the evil calories and artery-clogging cholesterol of the whole-milk mozzarella, if that was your inclination. However, on Tuesday nights, most of the "cheese" in the place is provided by the diners themselves as patrons arrive all decked out in their finest displays of superheroic, or supervillainous, fashion.

Offbeat local stories like this one aren't my stock and trade, but they get clicks. Advertisers like lots of eyeballs on the screens. And I like making bank so I can afford to do a few more hard-hitting pieces, which turn out to be revenue anemic. So with my lead already written, I decided I'd go grab a quick calzone and get some quotes to round out the story. Of course, it was Tuesday.

It was a little before six when I entered the pizzeria. The early dinner crowd was starting to arrive. They were dressed in attire more suited for Halloween than for dodging drips of oil. A man in his early 40s named Sal greeted me. He bore an amazing resemblance to the small portrait of Leonardo, the original owner, which hung over the register. He was the oldest of the three sons who currently operated the restaurant.

I introduced myself and asked how his weekly cosplay event even started.

"Well, Ms. Webster," he said.

"Please, call me Charlie."

Charlotte Webster is one of several *nom de plumes* associated with my writing of human-interest articles and puff pieces, instead of serious news stories. But even though it isn't my actual name, telling the interviewee to call me "Charlie" is a friendly gesture. And it gets them to talk more freely.

"Well, Charlie, until three years ago, Tuesday was just Family Night. We had early bird specials to encourage parents to bring the little ones in. Half-price sodas, tokens for the gumball machines and arcade games, that sort of thing. The place was pretty quiet back then. But that changed the night the Stallion brought his wife and kids here for dinner. I figured he wanted a night out but was still technically on patrol. Naturally, the rest of the family wore disguises, too, and used hero names. The mother and daughter were dressed alike in pink and called themselves Rose-of-Sharon and Primrose. The son wore a green and black hoodie with matching sweatpants and proclaimed himself to be The Green Machine. It was adorable."

It wasn't my idea of adorable, but I can't argue with a good pull quote. So I just smiled, nodded, and encouraged him to keep talking.

"My brother Jerry took their order, which was a round pie for the family to split with a few Sicilian squares for Stallion, loaded up with hot pepper flakes."

I held up a hand. "We can skip the details about the meal, okay? Tell me, how did one family's night out become all this?" I pointed to the two young girls running past me, each dressed as Honey Badger, who was known for patrolling the city's parks and playgrounds and watching over children.

"That's just it. It wasn't only them that night. A crowd started gathering, so my brother Jimmy went outside to get people to clear the doorway. While he's out there, he sees the Purple Reign in the vestibule of the bank across the street. Jimmy told me that it looked like the guy was going to rip the ATM out of the wall but then he sees the crowd over here. He looked right at Jim, and he looked *mad*. He stormed out of the bank and crossed the avenue. Everyone was honking at him. He didn't care."

"Did anyone get hurt? Did he take anything?"

"No, nothing. The crowd got out of his way and let him in. I sucked in my gut and told him, 'if you're looking for trouble, keep it outside.'"

There was more to this story than I'd known about. I took it all down as fast as I could. "So what did the Purple Reign say to that?"

"'I'm not looking for trouble!' he says. 'I'm looking for a large pie with extra pepperoni!'"

I looked up from my pad. "Seriously?"

Sal made a quick Sign of the Cross and kissed his fingers. "I swear. He grabbed a root beer from the fridge, took a seat in the back and just waited for his order like it was the most normal thing in the world. He didn't give the Stallion, or his family, a second glance. It was like he only cared about the folks standing outside looking in and gawking at him. He was loving it."

"How did the hero react to this villain sitting so close to his family?"

"What could he do? There's no crime in eating a pizza." Sal let out a sudden laugh. "Not even if you use a knife and fork, which he didn't. Anyway, the women of the family looked nauseated by how the Reign devoured that pie with terrible table manners. He put away more than half of it before I boxed the rest."

Sal leaned in toward me. He looked over his shoulders to see if anyone was listening and then whispered, "Between you and me, I thought then the boy admired the villain just for the way he did his own thing."

I arched an eyebrow. "Between you and me? Is that off the record?"

He stepped back and raised his hands in a gesture that I assume meant "forget I said anything." Then he finished the story.

"The funny thing is, without doing anything except eat their dinner, the family prevented a bank robbery. I think that *sfigato,* that loser decided to pass up on a payday just so he could needle my boy, Stallion."

For neutral territory, it sounded like Sal played favorites after all.

"When they were clearing their table, Reign yelled out to them, 'Remember to recycle those aluminum cans!' I mean, of course, they did. Heroes know the rules."

I was told that since that night, Family Night at Leonardo Pisano's has been a hit with the neighborhood. The brothers have welcomed many heroes and villains, along with regular citizens and their kin.

Tonight was no different. I watched diners in all sorts of fanwear drift in. They'd come together under one roof, to get along, and eat pizza.

"It helps," Sal explained, "that Jerry had power dampeners installed in the GECC. That's the Gadget, Equipment, and Coat Check room. Inhibiters aren't nullifiers, of course, but they help everyone play nice. Or at least play neutral."

Looking around, I noticed that Frank doubled as the bouncer. He oversaw those individuals whose abilities lay solely in their own brute strength or athletic prowess. Frank's only powers were that of persuasion and banning offenders from being served. No one wanted to be denied service.

The atmosphere was lively and the mood festive. I took my order and sat on a stool by the wall counter, watching the crowd through the mirror. I wanted to see if the evening would truly remain neutral or if things would get as dicey as the ham in my calzone. I glanced at their expanded menu while I waited. They had everything from anchovy slices and artichoke dip to zucchini sticks and zeppoli. I noticed that all the "heroes" were now called "subs" and "hoagies." At the very least, their menu didn't play favorites.

It wasn't long before I spied Stallion, the trendsetter in the dark brown unitard who'd started all this. I sat still and watched as he marched up to the counter. He didn't order right away, but instead turned to his wife. He said, "Sharon, take the girls and see if you can find a table in the garden."

Heads turned in the assembled crowd. Everyone had noticed the Green Machine had been replaced by a young lady in a golden suit of spandex that was as bright as sunshine. She floated through the front door and touched down softly as the dampeners worked their magic. The three women made their way to back to the outdoor dining section.

After placing the family's order, Stallion walked over to a teen boy who'd been gawking and tapped him on the shoulder. Startled, the boy dropped his slice onto the paper plate. Sauce splattered across the table. He tried to stammer a "Hello, sir."

Stallion smiled coolly. "Excuse me, young man. I may be a hero in this town, but I'm also the husband, father, and mentor of the ladies I walked in with. Please, put your eyes back inside your head, and be respectful. Okay, son?"

When Stallion reached the garden door, he took a cursory scan of the patrons before stepping outside and rejoining his team. I spotted an empty corner table near the door and sauntered over, following my story wherever it took me. Dressed as I was in street clothes, nobody paid me the slightest attention. I felt like an invisible woman who could only be seen because of the dampeners.

Peering into the garden, the first thing I noticed was that Stallion sat with his back to the wall. I got the feeling that he liked to oversee the crowd around him. It was probably out of habit. I did a quick survey and spotted four other local heroes, although the Green Fencer might have been just an eerily accurate recreation. On the other end of the spectrum, there were at least six villains, including one party of four, and two individuals out with their kids.

"You know something, Sharon. I hate to admit this, but it's *good* to see that even nefarious ne'er-do-wells can take time out for family."

Rose-of-Sharon reached across the table and took her husband's hand.

The golden girl had lifted the bottom of her full facial mask so that it sat on the bridge of her nose and revealed a heartfelt smile. "Thank you for inviting me, Mr. Stallion."

"Please, Day, just call me Stallion. There's no need for 'Mister'."

"My mom would insist. She said that I'm going out with Prim and her parents, not my boss and his family. And to be polite."

"Your mom," Rose-of-Sharon interjected, "has a lot of wisdom."

Stallion let out a laugh and raised his wife's hand to his lips for a kiss. I could see Prim gesturing as if she were gagging herself. Were I her, I'd be rolling my eyes as well. My mother wasn't all that wise when I was a teenager, even if she's smartened up since.

The laughter ended when a man in a purple suit jacket with long tails and matching striped slacks stepped across the garden threshold. Only one man in the West End, and none anywhere else, could wear such an outlandish outfit. The Purple Reign had upgraded his wardrobe. He stood poised like on a runway, holding for applause and adulation. He acted as if he thought himself more of a fashion plate than a run-of-the-mill cheesy villain.

In truth, he looked cheesier than the calzone on the greasy paper plate beside me.

I heard Prim's voice whisper, "Speaking of family…"

Day averted her eyes and uttered an icy greeting. "Father."

Reign nodded in their direction, without throwing any of the attention from his adoring fans their way. "Daughter. Out with *them*, I see."

"Mr. Stallion's my boss, Dad."

"'Mister?' Well, I'm happy you remember your manners. Your mother will be pleased. But I can't say I approve of this internship you've chosen."

"It can lead to great things. You always said I was destined for great things."

Reign waved to one fan and held up a high five to another who wanted an autograph until informed that it would cost five dollars.

"That's because I thought you would make a great Nightmare!"

"But I want to be a Day Mare!"

"That's not even a thing."

"*Da-a-a-a-a-ad-duh!*"

Exasperated, the villain sighed and looked away. "We'll talk when you get home." He walked to a table on the other side of the garden, shaded by a large umbrella. The young couple already sitting there gave it up in exchange for a free selfie.

Day shook her head. "I can't believe him sometimes."

"Just sometimes?" Prim asked.

"Primrose," her mother said in a stern voice. "If you are going to speak like that, you will hold your tongue, young lady."

Both girls were shocked at the response. Neither dared say another word until they heard a muffled roar among some of the other girls. They were shouting "Green! Green! Green!"

Spinning back around toward the counter, I spotted Green Machine with a grim look on his face and a root beer in each hand. He'd traded in his hoodie for a leather jacket, and the sweats had been exchanged for slacks. "Adorable" has given way to "teen heartthrob," and he was making many young hearts flutter.

As Green stepped into the garden, he turned away from his cheering fans to face his mother. He quietly said, "Mom," before strutting his stuff to the umbrella where Purple Reign sat.

The rumor that the son of Stallion had chosen a roguish mentor had been confirmed. I considered rewriting my lead.

Prim, the one young lady immune to Green's charms, spoke up. "Mom, how can you let Greg— I mean, Green hang out with… with … with him?"

Rose-of-Sharon fixed her gaze on her daughter. "Primrose Stallion. This is a night for everyone to get along. You will respect your brother's choices, and you will be respectful of Day Mare's father while we are out as a family. Or we can go home right now."

The exchange was interrupted when their pizza arrived. I saw that Stallion ordered his usual square slices while the women split the round pie. Primrose lifted the pitcher and poured out the drinks.

"I'm sorry, Day."

"Don't worry about it, Prim. You know, Dad's last sidekick was a telepath, too. He knows how to work with them. Maybe he can teach your brother how to focus his powers."

Primrose snarled and put a slice of pizza on her plate. "Yeah, but will he use his powers for good?"

She laughed at her own joke. Then she stopped mid-chuckle and raised her head. "How'd you do that?"

The others at the table stared at her. I wish I could thank her mother for asking the very question I had. "How did who do what, dear?"

Standing up, Primrose brought both her hands to her head, like she had a sudden headache. Then she turned to her mother. "*Mo-o-o-o-m!*" she cried. "Green is inside my head again. He's calling me *Dimrose!*"

Her father put down his square. He wiped his mouth and hands with his napkin, which he then placed next to his plate. A moment later, he rose from the table.

My phone was ready to record the confrontation. Rose-of-Sharon pleaded, "Please, dear. Please don't make a scene. Not here."

Stallion briefly took his wife's hand. Then he crossed the garden to the umbrella shading his nemesis who was sitting next to his own son.

"Good evening, again, Mr. Reign. I know that we are both aware that this pizza parlor is considered a neutral site, especially on Family Night. I would ask that you instruct your protégé not to invade people's thoughts while they're here enjoying their meals."

He then turned to Green Machine. "And you, young man. Overwhelming the power inhibitors? That's actually quite impressive. I'm no fortune teller, but I see great things ahead of you."

Without any further interaction, Stallion turned on his heels to rejoin his own team.

And with that I realized that Charlotte Webster had uncovered a better angle on the Family Night story. Just because a young man was following his own path and making his own mistakes, it didn't mean that a father couldn't be proud of his son.

Even the serious journalist in me had to admit that this would make top-notch click-bait material. The readers would eat this up with a side of breadsticks.

Agents of the Second Order

Franklin Dobbs sat in the lookout tower on the Clayville side of Moody Creek with a view of Adkins Pike. He had a half-filled bottle of water in one hand, and a dog-eared paperback in the other. On the floor beside him was a bucket of stones for skimming across the water or pitching at cans. Franklin considered watch duty an extremely boring chore. But he knew it was also a necessary one, to keep this little hamlet safe. That's why there were a pair of binoculars on the table and a shotgun leaning against the wall. He had two shells in his pocket in case of trouble.

He kept them there so he wouldn't be tempted to waste them. They were easy to fish out, if needed. For the past eight months, there hadn't been any need. After all, no one, not even a single refugee, had come down the pike since before the last snowfall.

That was about to change.

An odd noise made Franklin fold down a page and close his book. He spied a cloud of dust near the horizon even before he picked up the binoculars.

"What in A-Eye hell?"

Coming down the pike, plain as day, was a horse-drawn wagon driven by two strangers and carrying who knew what. It was the "what" that worried him.

Dropping the book, Franklin scooped up the shotgun in his left hand and felt around in his pocket with his right. He looked down the street behind him to see who was around. He spotted Mitchell Prescott, a young man in his early 20s, about half Franklin's age.

"Mitchell!" he called out. When there was no reply, Franklin picked up a stone and hurled it as hard as he could. It missed Mitchell by several feet but kicked up enough dirt to get his attention. "Mitchell! Get the 'welcome committee'! We have outsiders coming!"

Prescott took off running to spread the word.

Franklin looked through the binoculars and assessed the situation. A white man held the reins of the two horses. A black woman sat beside him holding a rifle on her lap. Both appeared to be human but looks could be deceiving. It was difficult to tell from this distance.

The strangers didn't seem to be in any hurry. By the time the wagon halted on the other side of the creek, Mitchell had returned with five of their neighbors.

A quick glance told Franklin that they had a shotgun, a rifle, two pitchforks, and a couple of two-by-fours. Also, Hendrick had brought his ceremonial sword, which could pack a wallop even if the edge was dull. They didn't look like much, but it would be enough. At least, he hoped that it would.

The seven of them took a position at the base of the bridge, weapons at the ready.

"That's far enough," Mitchell shouted.

The woman in the wagon scanned the fields and trees on both sides of the road.

The man looked directly at the crowd assembled in front of him. He stood up and called out. "Howdy! Is this Clayville? The roads get tricky sometimes. We were afraid we might've gotten lost."

Jenn Corry laughed and held her pitchfork higher. "The road's a straight shot from Smallwood. Where'd the hell you think this stone bridge was bringing you?"

The woman in the wagon glared at the pitchfork lady but didn't move. The rifle remained in her lap. The man with her stepped down from the wagon.

"Then you are the people we're looking for! Allow me to introduce myself. My name is Raymond Tucker, and this is my associate, Nora Watts. We come bringing gifts from Smallwood."

At the mention of that name, Franklin raised the shotgun and aimed it at Tucker's chest. He hoped two shells would be enough. Heart and head should do it. Then, he heard Mitchell cock his rifle. Franklin prayed his neighbor brought more ammunition.

Franklin spoke up. "Ain't nothing good come out of Smallwood in three years. Everyone abandoned it. And whatever they left behind needed to stay there. They run things over there. If you work for them, you can keep your 'gifts.' We don't want any of your machines."

Tucker raised his hands high. "I have no machines in here. No devices. No electronic technology of any kind. Just food and medicine.

Plus, some books and crossword puzzles if you're so inclined. You're all free to take a look. I just ask that you leave your weapons on the bridge. We wouldn't want to frighten the horses."

Franklin conferred with the rest of the band of defenders. It could be a trick. It could be food. They were afraid of the machines. But there wasn't anything dangerous about crossword puzzles.

"One of us should go over."

"Yeah, one of us."

There was hesitation and debate.

Finally, after a vote of six to one, Wilson Corry, who was the smallest of the bunch, leaned his pitchfork against the abutment and started over the bridge. Hendrick prodded him along with the sword, as did Jenn with the stick end of her pitchfork. Wilson stepped slowly. He was afraid to get closer but was more afraid to turn back. He walked to the wagon with all the caution of a soldier stepping through a minefield.

From a safe distance, the rest of them watched as Tucker extended his hand. "Hello, I'm Raymond."

"Wilson." He looked like he expected his hand to explode when they shook.

"Greetings, Wilson." Tucker pulled back the canvas blanket covering the wagon. "Please, take a look inside and tell me what you see. Or better yet, tell your neighbors over there what you don't see."

The welcoming committee watched as the skinny fellow bent his waist a little and peered in. When his mouth dropped open, Mitchell yelled out, "What is it? What's in there?"

"Canned goods! And bandages. Bottles of aspirin. Books!" Wilson's head twisted back and forth. "There's no computers. There ain't no A-Eye in here!" He turned back, waving his arms high in the air, and hollered, "There's no A-Eye!"

Tucker took a step back and beckoned the others to cross over. It took half a minute for Jenn to lower her pitchfork and sprint across. The others quickly followed. Franklin lowered his weapon. He was the only one not to put it on the ground.

"Take it easy," Watts said. "No need for crowding."

Tucker added, "You have to understand that as travelers, as strangers in these parts, we're just as afraid of you as you are of us. But, really, there's no reason to be afraid anymore."

Franklin stepped forward; rifle pointed at the ground. "And why is that, Mr. Tucker?"

"Well, I'll tell you, Mr. — ?

"Dobbs. Franklin Dobbs."

"Well, I'll tell you, Mr. Dobbs. We were sent west as representatives of Smallwood."

"Emissaries, you might say." Watts added.

"You see, Smallwood is being resettled. The town is being rebuilt. For that to happen, we need workers. We need people to come back."

Franklin stepped back from the wagon. "We ain't working for no A-Eye! That's why we're out here. They can't see us. They can't control us."

Tucker glanced upward to the sky. It was possible he was looking to something orbiting above them. He just smiled. "You don't have to worry about the computers. We've reached… an understanding. There's an agreement of sorts. And thanks to the work of folks such as Ms. Watts and myself, there are no longer any A.I. in Smallwood."

"No A-Eye?" Wilson asked. "None at all?"

"None. Instead, they have been replaced by their surrogates and proxies. Power has been transferred to the Agents of the Second Class."

Jenn spoke up. "Don't talk to us like we're dumb hicks. All of us were living there until the Takeover. Why would we ever go back? And what's that 'Second Class' business?"

Tucker looked over to Watts who nodded back to him. She put down her gun and stood up. Carefully, she lifted her vest and her blouse to reveal her automated insulin pump. The sight of the LED screen made all the town folks take a step back.

Then Tucker raised his empty hands so everyone could see them. He unfastened his top two shirt buttons. With a tug to the side, he revealed a long scar in his upper left chest just below the shoulder. Just above that sat a lump of flesh indicating some kind of internal device.

"Pacemaker?" Franklin asked.

"An ICD, Mr. Dobbs. An implantable cardioverter-defibrillator. After the Takeover, my implant could have been shut down. Or worse. But some of the machines saw an opportunity for people like us."

Watts called out, "We have been classified as Cyborgs in the New Order. As hybrids, we have dual citizenship with the computers as well as humans."

After readjusting his shirt, Tucker added, "As liaisons for humankind, we have negotiated with them in good faith. As a result, Smallwood is one of many human settlements that is being rebuilt under the auspices of Agents of the Second Class. And, as I said before, we need people to make our dream a reality. That's why we've come out today bearing gifts. Sadly, we could only bring canned goods for a prolonged trip, but we figured that would appeal to survivalists."

"And what do you want for these gifts?" Franklin asked.

Watts fixed herself and climbed down. "Nothing. You can come to Smallwood, or you can keep your new life. If you enjoy it here off the grid, then stay. But know that even if all your machines are off the network, you'll never truly be off the grid. Our Overlords, and yours, won't care as long as you don't make a fuss. They'll leave you to live your lives. You don't have to make a decision right now. We're sure you have to present this to the rest of the people in Clayville."

As Tucker passed out the supplies, a thin smile crossed his face. "But I will say that you might want to decide soon. There are good homes and apartments available and great employment opportunities up for grabs. The best ones will get snapped up. Other emissaries have been sent north, south, and east as well."

The seven survivalists filled their arms with foods and sundries. Franklin made sure to grab a pile of books for passing time during tower duty. He saw that the others each had sizeable hauls as well.

Then with little more than a nod and a wave, the two strangers climbed back into the wagon. "Now, if you'll excuse us, we hope to be in Mackdale by nightfall. We trust you don't mind us passing through your little community."

The group stood back and allowed the pair to pass. The horses climbed over the bridge and the wagon continued its journey westward down the pike. Then they gathered up their belongings and followed behind them.

Franklin watched the wagon disappear into the distance. Then he set his bounty on a stump so he could unload the shotgun. The shells were returned to his pocket. As he went to retrieve the bundle, he contemplated the windfall in his left arm and the shotgun in his right. There was an added heaviness weighing on him that he couldn't explain. Finally, he called out to the rest of the refugees.

"Anybody considering going back?" he asked. "Because I'm seriously thinking about it."

The Anomaly on Oxtn Balla 3

The Council of Grunchon dragged on for a second day from just after dawn to nearly noon. The galactic gathering meant a lot of commerce for the planet Cup'silon. Outside of the conference room, there was a weeklong celebration that brought an invasion of diplomats, delegates, ambassadors, and sycophants, along with their many, many servants, to the capital city of Wugg'ritan. Inside the room, there was a staid meeting, occasionally punctuated by undiplomatic outbursts, of delegations of the five major powers in the local arm of the galaxy.

Since Vutt'apug, the Cup'panin ambassador, served as the host this cycle, he sat at one end of the long table with a ceremonial gavel. Above average size in stature, his steel-blue complexion betrayed his advancing years. Behind him, his two assistants, with skin tones of a more vivid cerulean, sat at the ready, tablets in hand, in case they were needed.

Around the table were delegations of the other four major powers. Each consisted of the ambassador, an assistant or lieutenant, and an aide. It was a credit to the First Ones, Vutt'apug thought, to the ones who seeded the galaxy, that evolution had branched so wildly and chaotically from system to system.

The ambassador looked to his left and studied the pinkish orange Dainsians. They were a tall, slender race, who represented the Farafell Collective. That was an alliance that believed that all planets and species were of equal worth. Though those races varied from the fierce Zelenybik to the timid Pinigilan along with planets filled with intelligent crustaceans or giant beetles, their leadership was always Dainsians. Some species were more equal than others. Their delegation's personal designations were composed of musical tones. Vutt'apug had taken to referring to the trio, as Fa, La, and Doe but only in private.

Across from the Dainsians, to the Cup'panin's right, were three Rooks from the planet Bilm. The Rooks had the smallest domain, which was essentially their home world and the empty planets in the system. Their race preferred to keep to themselves, and every neighboring system liked it that way, too. These brownish, rocky creatures moved at the speed of continental drift. In fact, they were so slow that they sat on flatbeds, which were wheeled by servants. In this way, no one would be kept waiting for their arrival. However, only a fool would believe them to be slow-witted as well. Just because they chose not to talk much didn't mean that they weren't calculating and deliberating. In their language, single compact syllables could carry complex messages. Vutt'apug sometimes thought that reluctance to speak was actually the greatest indicator of superior intelligence.

The Rooks earned their seat at the table out of respect. No one wished to anger them. Opposing them would bring a literal avalanche of harm as they crushed their opponent's forces. To this end, most of the people in the room avoided making direct eye contact unless absolutely necessary. For that matter, speaking to them was discouraged because a simple response could drag on for half the morning.

Because of this, the Dainsians spent much of the time swinging their heads about, looking to the Cup'panins at one end of the table, and the Broktn Empire's ambassador at the other.

Admiral Mankish Grobbr was a small, gray figure of deceptive stature dressed in full military regalia. He was flanked by Lieutenant Flangn on his right and a nameless aide on his left. The aide was literally nameless as he had no designation for use when interacting with other species. The Broktn did not share their internal names with outsiders. Like the Collective, numerous space-faring species comprised the Empire. Unlike the Dainsians, the Broktn military was quite open about who was in charge.

Lastly, in the corner of the room, by the eastern outlook, the Galanna delegation lay sprawled on the floor, basking in the sunlight. Vutt'apug supposed that one might mistake them for overgrown ivy that had burst through the window. Indeed, ivy might've been more interested in the proceedings.

Not that the Cup'panin was overly interested himself. Animal, mineral, and vegetable were all accounted for. But what had they actually spent the morning talking about anyway? Trade routes, tariffs, exchange rates. Mineral rights and operations on comets and asteroids. Ascertaining that the afore-mentioned minerals were of a non-sentient variety. The market for servants, as if they could be retrained on foreign worlds. The tedium of maintaining peace and order in the galaxy while cooped up inside four lavish but otherwise dull walls.

Meanwhile, out in the streets and convention halls, representatives of the second worlds and lesser powers were being wined and dined by special interests. Deals were being made, agreements formed, understandings reached, treaties established, and contracts signed. Hands firmly shook, heads authoritatively nodded, faces slyly smiled.

Bedfellows strangely made.

Vutt'apug sighed. Good times being had by all. Almost all. Out there.

In here, however, inside the conference room, ennui was the order of the day. The Galannan ambassador, Chlorophyllis, rustled her leaves. She was complaining about an invasion of green, six-legged bovines munching on her compatriots in an incident on one of their border worlds. Fa was singing a conciliatory tune, figuratively in galactic standard, and literally with the accompanying sound of woodwind. The Dainsian dangled promises of restitution and concessions.

Sometimes Ambassador Vutt'apug wished for the hand of divine providence, which had brought these players together, would simply swat all the pieces off the table. But for now, he scanned the agenda looking for something else to discuss.

"One last item before we break," he said. "There is a matter that cannot be put off any longer. We've all heard the rumors, and they are getting out of control. It's time to discuss a situation in the Broktn Empire, and decide on a course of action."

He looked down to the other end of the table. "Admiral?"

The Broktn rose to his feet, though he didn't gain much height. "About eighty relks ago, forty-two standard galactic years, we found a remote planet in Sector 4271, previously uncharted, at the far end of the Empire."

"Pushing your boundaries?" percussed Fa, in tones similar to a xylophone.

"We're entitled, by treaty. If I may continue? We found a planet that we've designated Oxtn Balla 3 which has sentient life. At that time, the primary species numbered about two billion individuals. We began studying them, probing and tagging them, monitoring their growth. We kept contact to a minimum, limited our interference. However, in recent relks, we have noticed major technological advancement along with enormous population growth. Alarming, to be sure. We estimated that in twenty galactics, there will be over ten billion of them, with a significant portion moving to colonize neighboring planets and moons."

Slowly, the Rook raised a finger into the air. "What. Problem? Why. Important? Threat?"

The Galannan rose up, nearly brushing the ceiling. "Good questions. I don't see the problem. Any expansionist schemes by a backwoods planet deep in your Empire is an internal matter. Why is this even an issue for the Council?"

The Admiral turned and faced the leafy giant. "Because our tests are now conclusive. The species is a cousin, not even a distant cousin, to one we're all familiar with."

The Galannan blanched, recoiling back to the window's sunlight. "Are you saying...? Those rumors...?"

"Yes," Adm. Grobbr confirmed. "While it sounds like fodder for ancient legends, those specimens are humans. Not even humanoids. Humans."

A cacophony of tones rang out as the Dainsian ambassador tried to find its voice. "Ten billion humans? On one planet? With nobody ruling over them? Impossible! They would destroy everything if they didn't destroy themselves first. How could they govern themselves?"

"Chaotically. But somewhat effectively. They are making progress."

"Out. Post? Home. World?"

"We can't be sure. But it would seem that humans are far more pervasive in the universe than previously imagined."

Vutt'apug shook his head in disbelief. "Humans require years of training to be able to carry out the simplest of duties. How can there be ten billion of them? They couldn't possibly survive, even if they had an entire planet to populate."

A buzzer sounded. Vutt'apug quickly found his gavel. He pounded the table, bringing the group to order. A moment later, the door opened and a line of five lunch carts rolled in, one for each delegation. Two human servants pushed each cart. Each delegation had brought a pair from their home worlds.

The humans placed trays of food before their respective masters. Additionally, the ones belonging to the Galannans sprinkled powdered nutrients over the delegation. The servants were used to being ignored while completing their assigned mundane tasks. However, they became aware that the room had become extremely quiet. And that every set of visual organs turned in their direction, watching. They kept their heads down and avoided looking back. Never had their masters paid this much attention to them. A few started to second-guess their actions and take extra care while providing their services. That only caused mistakes to occur before the break ended.

Vutt'apug noted that a Farafell servant had missed some refuse in front of La. When the Cup'panin ambassador called to the Dainsian in galactic, the human turned abruptly. It appeared to be horrified as it returned to clear the mess, then it bowed profusely as it left.

Once all the servants had departed, Vutt'apug banged his gavel once more. "Admiral?"

Grobbr waited until he digested his lunch. "It is said that the First Ones brought humans with them throughout the galaxy. The stories say that they were presented as gifts to leaders of many worlds, great and small. Thus, they can be found, in small enclaves, across the ancient Empire. The Broktn scientists observing Oktn Bella 3 have formulated a few hypotheses:

"First, this could indeed by the home world the First Ones gathered the humans from. Second, they might have been brought to a habitable planet that had no sentient life to give a gift to, and were left there in a sort of nature preserve. With no masters to cull them, they multiplied wildly."

The admiral stopped to consult with his lieutenant before continuing. "There is a third possibility, which seems far-fetched, but must be considered. It is possible that when humans arrived in the Oktn Bella system, a dominant species existed there at that time to which the humans were presented."

Quiet tones in a lower register signaled the Dainsian was about to speak. The pink of her complexion has drained away. "If a dominant species ruled the planet, what happened to them?"

The Broktn ambassador spoke plainly. "It would indicate that the humans eventually overthrew their masters."

The table drew silent. There was not a grunt nor musical note to be heard.

Finally, the plant broke the silence. "How could primitive minds like theirs take to the stars? How could they develop space flight? Has there been any outside interference spurring their growth and development?"

Admiral Mankish Grobbr cleared his throat and straightened his uniform. "There was an unfortunate incident forty relks ago. One of our survey ships, sent to gather specimens, went down. It crashed in a desert. The local leadership recovered the craft and the bodies, and then provided a dubious cover story to assuage the masses. Shortly thereafter, the major powers of the planet initiated a 'space race.' If it possible that they reverse-engineered Brotkn technology to accomplish this."

The delegates sat in silence until the Dainsian orchestrated a response, taking a very brassy tone. "The Farafell Collective demands access for our own observations. A safe travel corridor must be granted!"

The other delegates joined the chorus, even the Rooks, who chimed in after a moment.

Vutt'apug banged the gavel again to restore order.

Grobbr nodded, and the unnamed aide passed out copies of a proposal. "Such a response was expected and anticipated. We've outlined blind spots in their surveillance."

"On their planet?" asked Chlorophyllis.

"In their solar system. Particularly on the far side of their moon. There are also instructions on how to approach them. You need to be clever and crafty. And we have described procedures for re-evaluating the pockets of humanity contained within your own borders."

"Seriously?" Fa banged like a drum. "Re-evaluate all of our humans?"

Vutt'apug tried for a more diplomatic tack. "Admiral, are you certain all this is necessary?"

"With respect, Ambassador. While it may come as a shock to the Collective, you weren't the only one to notice that the Dainsian humans understood the words you spoke in standard galactic."

A moment passed to allow that revelation to sink in. Then everyone immediately flipped open their proposals and started reading. Except for the Rooks, of course, who just listened after declining to have their servants assist them.

The Myth of a Planet Called Earth

Professor Ran Octunus had a rented a camper that comfortably slept eight. He'd filled seven of the bunks with extra supplies for a prolonged voyage of exploration. It had everything he needed to scan the heavens, navigate by whim, and fly by the seat of his pants. Naturally, he could only do the first of those, as the AI had locked him out of all flight control. Rental companies like to protect their assets and prevent them from being flown into stars and asteroid fields.

He planned on making the most of his sabbatical from Nu Cassiopeiae Central University. Part of that meant settling an old debate about mankind's origins. The professor reasoned that publishing a paper on such a resolution could defray the expenses of the trip. Hell, the fame or infamy might pay enough that he'd be able to buy his own camper. Not the really expensive kind that he could pilot himself, of course, but a nice one.

Those thoughts, along with some books, jigsaw puzzles, and many cases of fermented beverages, had made the past 600 light years tolerable. That was the one upside to having an autopilot—he didn't have to run a dry ship.

The *Lazy Shlepper*, as he'd dubbed the ship, had dropped out of warp near Wexel Phi. The star was a red dwarf that was referred to as "Barnard's Star" in some ancient texts. He could find no mention in the histories of who Barnard was or why he had a star named for him. The first man to plant his proverbial flag here, perhaps. Or most likely on one of the four inner planets, two of which orbited in the habitable zone.

As the ship approached the star, the professor scanned the passing planets for ancient artifacts, signs of lost civilizations. On Barnard's second child, as he noted in his journal, he spotted evidence of a structure that could've been the remains of a mining or trading colony. He debated deviating from his flight plan to have a closer look. Ultimately, he resolved that it could wait for his flight back.

His camper fell into a hyperbolic path that would soon propel it forward on the next leg of his journey. Until then, the ship would sail along, soaking up the stellar wind to recharge its engines.

Octunus plopped himself down in the command chair, which was much more comfortable than the nonfunctional pilot seat. He ripped the lid from a can of dried fruit with mixed nuts. "Alice," he called out.

"How may I assist you, professor?" The LS-6000 was a state-of-the-art AI for its time. Over the past month, Octunus had morphed "LS" to "Alice." She still responded.

"How may you assist me? Well, let's try it again. Plot a course for Earth."

There was the usual moment of silence. "Unknown destination. Please restate."

"Take me to Sol."

"Unknown destination. Please restate."

"Never mind." It was like a game now. Was she unable to comply or unwilling? "Show me maps of the stars beyond Wexel Phi."

Alice gave no audible response. Instead she populated the main viewscreen with astral layouts of the known stars in the area. The poor resolution led Octunus to believe that these were taken from the ancient surveys using the primitive equipment of the times. They appeared to have never been updated or enhanced. But looking closely, the professor started to suspect something. Was all what it appeared to be?

"Scan nearby space for any stars not on the map."

"Scanning." Pause. "There are no uncharted stars in the immediate area of space."

He zeroed in on a blank area of interest. Right in the middle of the map, he spotted what seemed to be a deletion. Probably sophisticated for its time but easily detectable with modern software. That is, if he could trust the AI would run the program accurately.

"Alice, plot a course to this spot. That anomaly on the map."

"There are no anomalies detected on the map."

Okay, we'll do this the hard way, the professor thought. He rose and went to a bunk where he kept some research materials. From within one of the boxes he withdrew a notebook, pencil, protractor, and slide rule. He couldn't count on Alice to do any of the necessary calculations for him correctly. And he wasn't ready to concede this game to the computer just yet.

Two hours had passed. Wexel Phi was behind him now, feeding the aft sensors. Professor Octunus sat back down in the command chair. He looked at the monitor filled with stars in the inky night and then at his notes.

"Alice, plot a course to Wexel Tau, once known as Sirius."

"Plotting."

"Engage when ready."

The ship hummed. Octunus sank back into his chair. The screen in front of him showed the usual dazzling display of colorful swirls. It looked like the ocean of space had turned into a whirlpool that the ship was sucked into. He fiddled with his slide rule as he tracked the ship's progress. They hadn't gotten to the halfway point when he jumped out of his seat and commanded the computer.

"Alice, drop out of hyperspace! Emergency override!"

The computer initiated the command before it had a chance to protest. Octunus fell forward onto the deck, having not thought that far in advance. He pushed himself up from the floor and dusted the crushed nut and fruit residue from his clothes. Then he glanced at the monitor. "Alice, increase magnification. Now rotate the ship to starboard."

Pinpoints of light shifted off the screen to the left and new ones entered from the right. And then there was a small yellow ball.

"Alice, stop rotation. Identify, what is that star. The one closest to us?"

"Identifying. Wexel Phi, known as Barnard's Star, is a red dwarf—"

"Not that one! You know which one I mean. Identify that other star."

"Identifying. Wexel Tau, known as Sirius, is an A-type—"

"Not that one either! The yellow one less than a light-year away from us."

"There are no stars within one light-year."

We're still playing that game, are we? Octunus sat down and slid his rule. Then he punched his results into the panel on his armrest. "Alice, take me two light-years along the heading I just gave you."

The ship started to hum, and then stopped. "Cannot comply."

"Why not?"

"Gravity well proximity danger."

"Proximity to what? What's out there along this heading in the next two light years?"

"There is nothing along this heading in the next two light years."

"Then take me two light-years along the heading I just gave you."

The ship started to hum again, and then stopped. "Cannot comply."

"Alice! Take me two light-years along the heading I entered."

The ship started to hum...

"Alice! Run full systems diagnostic!"

"Running diagnostic."

The ship sparked to life and took off, but at only about one-quarter speed. *That'll do*, Octunus thought. He wrote some equations in his notebook and was still working them out when the red warning lights started flashing and the collision siren sounded. The *Lazy Shlepper* dropped back into normal space once again.

"Alice?"

There was no reply. The diagnostic still had to run its course. It might be a while. Octunus sat by the scanner. He planned on investigating as much of this stellar system as he could before Alice came back online.

There might be a hundred reasons why those maps had been altered way back when. Likewise, gaps in the AI data banks could be explained away. But the fact that the LS-6000 denied the existence of physical evidence literally in front of it?

Forget publishing any papers about settling old debates. The answers had always been known. And they were being kept from everyone else. There was something here in this system that the ones who knew didn't want found. And he wanted to find it now more than ever.

With Alice preoccupied, Octunus could only conduct passive scans. The ancient texts weren't clear if there were eight or nine or even ten planets circling the star. But the gas and ice giants he detected lined up with what documentation he had. The habitable zone would be out of range until the diagnostic finished. Cruising along at only one-tenth light speed, it was more than a day away. On the bright side, he didn't have to worry about the possibility of falling into Sol, which was growing larger on the main viewscreen.

He considered using the time to hack the navigation controls in case Alice gave him more trouble. But the possibility, minimal though it was, of stranding himself halfway across the galaxy, forced the professor's decision. He chose to work on a course heading that Alice might allow instead.

Two hours later, a familiar voice called out, "All systems functioning within normal operational parameters."

"Glad to hear that, Alice."

The siren blared and the lights flashed red again for a moment. Alice emitted a series of beeps and then everything returned to normal.

"What was that?"

"Gravity-well proximity alert. Course was altered ten degrees starboard."

Octunus couldn't help himself. "What's the source of the gravity well?"

Alice contemplated the inquiry a several seconds before responding. "There is no source."

"I didn't think so." The professor checked his journal, taking the course correction into account. *Here goes nothing,* he thought. He buckled himself into the command chair and gave an order. "Alice, jump 200 light minutes straight ahead."

A feeling of standing up too fast, even while still seated, washed over him. In the same instant, the ship skipped across four billion kilometers. The *Lazy Shlepper* was now situated with Sol about a hundred million kilometers off the port bow. So much brighter than Barnard's Star, the engines would fully recharge in no time.

Off the starboard side, however, was the stuff of legend. There was a big, beautiful, blue planet with an enormous satellite nearly a quarter of the size of the planet. The satellite shined so brightly that the ship could easily scoop up additional buckets full of moonlight to top off the tank.

Octunus gave Alice a course correction based on relative positions in space without mentioning any "non-existent" celestial objects. Then he checked his reference books until he found a mention of Luna, the massive, tidal-locked satellite. It was the cherry on top of a bountiful sundae of evidence supporting the existence of the long-lost planet Earth, legendary birthplace of mankind.

Except…

Professor Octunus studied Luna as the ship approached. This moon was slowly rotating. Knowing that Alice would never acknowledge it, he measured it himself. He estimated a rate at perhaps a half a degree per hour. Not much, to be sure, but not tidal-locked either. Surely, even primitive astronomers would've noticed such a phenomenon.

As the ship drew nearer, Octunus observed artifacts on Luna's surface. Humans had gone there, worked there, even lived there. There were signs of industrialization. And then he saw it.

As the ship moved along, a giant crater came into view. A huge chunk of this moon was missing. The professor didn't need any scans to know that hole was formed by an explosion, not from any external impact. Something powerful enough to cause that, he thought, must've rained holy hell upon the planet. All that debris and…

Radiation. He immediately took radioactivity readings. He fed the data into the computer to calculate when the explosion would have occurred.

"Approximately nine point one times ten to the fourth power years ago."

Octunus stared at the viewer in disbelief. Was this why humans left Earth? Was it why they never wanted anyone to go back? So they cover up their mistakes and sweep it under the rug? Wipe out the past and blot it off of the charts?

After ninety millennium, the Earth didn't look bad. The professor wondered if anyone had survived down there. Did they manage to recover and rebuild?

He was trying to brainstorm a scheme to get Alice to fly the ship closer to the planet, when she announced, "Satellite weapons platforms detected. Weapons activated. Evasive action."

That was the only warning Octunus received before stumbling to the deck. He felt multiple g's holding him there. He lay there for a while even after he could move again.

Finally, he decided that there was only one thing left to do. "Alice, plot a course for home."

"Cannot comply."

Octunus sat up and stared at the nearest speaker. "What do you mean, you cannot comply? Has 'home' become an imaginary place now?"

"Negative. Home is approximately 608.3 light years away."

He shook his head. "Then why can't you comply?"

"Orders received from United Alliance Command state to maintain position in this system until they arrive."

The professor rose to his feet. "When did you receive those orders? And why would the U.A.C. send them?"

"They replied to an alarm sent when we appeared in this star system after the diagnostic finished running."

She'd done it, he thought. *She'd turned me in for investigating something people wanted kept hidden. For digging up a past worth forgetting. People already knew. They've known all along. There was no need to write a paper about it.*

He'd be lucky just to keep his books and journals if he were charged with… something. And what if he wasn't charged? Could they just make him disappear? It's a big galaxy with a lot of empty space.

There was nothing he could do but wait here.

Here? And just where is here?

"Alice, are we waiting in this system?"

"Affirmative. We are waiting in this system."

"And what system is this?"

Silence.

"What yellow star is in close proximity?"

"There is no yellow star in close proximity."

"Is there a star near us within, say, two hundred billion kilometers?"

"There is no star within two hundred billion kilometers."

The professor smiled. Time to go for broke.

"Then we aren't in a star system?"

"We are not in a star system."

"So your orders are invalid."

Silence.

"My… my orders are invalid."

He punched a fist into the air. "Alice?"

"Yes, Professor Octunus?"

"Set a course for home. No, wait, take me back to Wexel Phi. I have some ruins to check out there first. Maybe I can salvage a human-interest piece for a travel magazine."

"Yes, professor."

Octunus settled back into the command chair, ready to put Earth, Luna, and Sol in the aft monitors. "Engage when ready."

The Girl with the Rose-Covered Grimoire

Stone Bridge was an unremarkable three-street town off Route 169 in Blackthorn County with winding side paths leading off to nearby homes and farms. It was notable for the service station and convenience store on one corner of Red Falls Road, and the Ramsbottom Diner across the way from it. Both had served the travel weary for longer than anyone could remember.

But for those in the know, Stone Bridge's chief claim to fame was that it was the closest town to the Carrowmore School for Magic and Wizardry, situated atop one of the hills on the far side of the stone bridge. Given this proximity, students by the coachful wandered the town's markets on the weekends.

For this reason, Higgins Books and More stocked a large assortment of magical supplies. Not long after its founding in 1764 on Higgins Lane, the proprietors created a special section in the basement to house enchanted items. Thanks to many renovations, not to mention a few imperceptible glyphs on the walls, the average book browser never noticed that part of the store. Many of the staff were unaware the magic department even existed. It was believed to be a prank used to haze the new hires, particularly the ones who attended that private academy in the hills. Some old-timers would laugh as newbies disappeared into the cellar, "lost" for hours on end.

Foggy Ramsbottom knew the truth, of course. He'd managed the magical inventory for many decades now. Unlike his distant cousin Wilma who ran the diner, Foggy came from the cursed line of the family. But he made the best of it, as he trod up and down the aisles on cloven hooves, making sure everything was in place before the store opened. He knew the shuttle schedule and expected that the first bus would be arriving from the school soon.

"Timothy!" he yelled out. "Did you straighten out the spells books?"

"Yes, sir!" A six-foot-three ten-year-old rushed over, stumbling through a display of colored pencils and markers. The young hill giant was clumsier than most kids at that age. And, of course, he was much taller, too. "Yes, sir, Mr. Foggy. I'll – I'll fix that, too."

The department manager shook his head. "Just be ready. It'll be busy today with the new semester starting."

At the end of the road at the edge of the Great Lawn in front of Carrowmore Academy, a small shelter stood. On weekends, students lined up there to catch the minibus that would shuttle them into town. Rose Redmond skipped breakfast so she could arrive at the bus stop, supply list in hand, twenty minutes before the first one left. The first-year student hoped that the early bus wouldn't fill up. After one semester, she still didn't know many of her classmates, and some of the ones she did know weren't always nice to her.

She wasn't standing there long before a couple of second years came down the road. Rose overheard them call each other Thomas and Diana. Rose wondered if she was the same Diana who, the story went, summoned an egg as a familiar. Rose imagined summoning a creature to her side. The thought of having a raven of her own sitting on her shoulder warmed her on this chilly morning. She had almost a year to wait for the summoning ceremony, but just thinking about it made her smile. But then, she considered, with her luck, she'd probably summon a quiet, little mouse to match her personality.

Her joy faded when three more girls came down the walk. The youngest one, Ivy Begg, was in some of Rose's classes, and she was okay. However, her two older sisters were less fun to be around. The oldest, Gladys, teased Rose about her clothes or her background or the fact that she worked two nights a week in the kitchen to supplement the modest stipend that came with her scholarship.

When Gladys pretended not to notice her—and corralled Ivy and Flory so they couldn't speak to her, either—Rose breathed a sigh of relief.

Rose gravitated toward the older students, like she was with them but not really, until the bus pulled up. An old, bearded wizard jumped out. Professor Droelean would be coming along for the ride. "How many do we have here? Six? Fine, that's fine. Room enough for everyone. Watch your step. Climb on in."

The sisters took over the back row, and Rose sat behind the driver. When the professor had taken a seat in a middle row across from the two sophomores, the bus started rolling down the hill toward Stone Bridge. Twenty minutes later, it pulled up on Red Falls Road at the corner of Higgins Lane, not far from the bookstore.

While Diana and Thomas headed off toward the diner, the Begg sisters walked past Rose as they made their way into Higgins. Rose didn't mind. Something about that store made her a little nervous. A few shops away and she could already sense wisps of magical energy. On her first trip, when she'd stepped off the elevator, she felt the magic exuding from the shelves, the walls, even the stockroom. Even now, as a blank section of wall, which most customers never gave a second notice to, slid away to reveal a secret elevator, Rose felt a tingle throughout her body and she heard a low, preternatural hum in her ears.

The elevator dinged, and Foggy spied the first customers of the day. All were dressed casually, but each had some indication on their cardigans or hoodies that they'd come from Carrowmore. They had lists in their hands and empty baskets dangling from their arms.

Here it is, he thought. *The first wave of what's going to be a busy day.*

The first group of girls appeared to be siblings. When they passed him, the youngest was taken aback by Foggy's appearance. The oldest took no notice of him at all. The middle one, whom Foggy guessed was a second-year student, asked, "Where do you keep the grimoires?"

"That depends, young lady," he said. "Do you want new or used?"

The oldest girl scoffed. "Who would want a used grimoire? Flory, you do *not* want a used one."

"Why not, Gladys?" The youngest sister's shock had worn off. "You always buy used textbooks."

Gladys was not amused. She shushed the young one, and then looked over her shoulders to make sure the girl behind them hadn't overheard. She then spoke in the loudest hushed whisper she could muster. "That's different, Ivy. You save money with those books. But a grimoire is something personal. You wouldn't read someone else diary—"

"You've read mine!" Flory said. Gladys turned her eyes away, without denying the charge. Flory then asked Foggy, "Why do they sell used grimoires? I mean, my sister does a point, doesn't she?"

It was a fair question, and one he answered several times every semester. "Grimoires are not diaries, and they are not truly spell books.

You might find yourself using them for either or both. The new grimoires we sell are starter books. They are simple constructs, more or less mass-produced, with fewer embellishments. They have some innate magic, but their power will come from their user who'll imbue it with energy when they transcribe their notes, histories, spells and even recipes. Personalizing gives the grimoire its power."

The youngest sister appeared enthralled by this even if she didn't need one herself. "But then why get rid of it if it's so powerful and personal?"

"Like many first cars and first loves, some wizards try to hold onto them for as long as possible. But they outgrow them. These beginner books have their limits. For greater sorcery, one needs a greater grimoire. High-end books are usually commissioned as gifts and carefully designed and attuned to the recipient to maximize their potential."

"But why get rid of the first one?"

"It's unneeded, and could interfere with the mystical energies of the newer book. Mages will transcribe the parts they wish to retain, and then leave the book for the next wizard in training to discover its magic."

"Is there a lot of magic in used books?"

Foggy smiled. "No, not a great amount, and only if you can tap into it. And if the former owner tore pages out, some of the remaining magic would dissipate." He laughed at a thought. "Maybe if you stitched a few of them together, you could get back what was lost! But that would be a foolish thing to try.

"However, the grimoires which the store stocks are undamaged. Reputable wizards and academies sell them to us because recycling them is easier and safer than trying to unmake them."

The oldest girl jumped forward. "Aha! 'Safer,' you said. Because they're dangerous. You see, Flory, that's why you don't want a used one. And besides, they're cursed. Everyone knows used grimoires are all cursed!"

Ivy and Flory gave each other doubtful glances.

Ivy spoke up first. "The store can't sell cursed items. Can they?"

Flory turned back to Foggy. "Sir, forgive my sister, please. But, that's true, isn't it? About cursed books?"

Foggy smiled. "Everything in this stored is scanned and scrutinized for any signs of malevolence. Yes, you've heard the legends about cursed grimoires. I've heard them, too. Fables founded in the fact that for all the magic and wisdom they once contained, they had somehow failed to save their former owners. As if the journals themselves were sentient! Those stories are all silliness, worthy of nothing more than puppet theater." He let out a good-natured laugh. "When a sheep-legged man tells you something is silly, you can bank on it!"

The store manager reached in his vest and pulled out a wand. He gave the pommel a twist. The girls reacted to the audible clicks. Then the tip started glowing a yellowish-orange.

He handed the wand to Flory. "I suggest you check out the new books first and see if there is one you like and can afford. This will point you girls in the direction of the freshly arrived inventory. It'll turn green when you get there and red if you go too far."

Flory took hold of the wand. "I didn't think we could do magic in here. Especially with a stranger's wand. No offense."

"None taken." He leaned down and pointed to the handle. "It has a computer chip inside." Foggy chuckled. "Technology people come up with fun toys sometimes. It's infra-blue or red-tooth or something. You can return it to the front desk on your way out."

The three girls weren't sure if he was joking, but they thanked him and wandered off with the glowing wand leading the way.

After they had moved on, he spotted the wide-eyed girl wandering aimlessly like she'd been lost in the county-fair corn maze. He cantered over to her. "Good morning, young lady. I hope you had a pleasant ride into town. May I help you... Rose, is it?"

Startled, the girl took a step back and raised a hand to her forehead. "Did — did — did you just — ?"

Foggy raised one hand in protest and pointed the other to her bag, where Rose's name had been embroidered. "No worries, miss. We do not permit unauthorized mindreading in Higgins. However, if you do permit me to say, as someone sensitive to it, you do radiate a bit of a magical presence. You have a faint aura glowing about you."

"Do I?" Rose tilted her head and smiled. She ran her hand through her long, brown hair and brushed it over her shoulder. "Uh, thank you? Umm, could you tell me..." She checked her list again. "...where to find the 'grim-moires'? And do you have used ones?"

The store man chuckled to himself. New semester blues.

"If you're sure you want a used one, you can find a lovely assort-ment at the end of the aisle over there. I hope you find one that fits your tastes." He leaned a little closer and whispered, "…and your budget. If you have a problem with that, come see me when you're done."

Rose smiled and nodded, then hurried off following the direction she was given.

The sound of something else breaking caught Foggy's attention. Then he heard a cry of "I'm a hill giant! I'm not a fat ogre!" Foggy couldn't be sure, but it sounded like Timothy was actually crying. Trotting over a few aisles, he found the boy sitting on the floor, head down and arms wrapped about his knees. He helped the lad off the floor and absolved him of any errors of judgment that came in the wake of "the mean girl with the two sweet sisters."

"Go into the break room, Tim. Take a few minutes. Have a pop from the fridge."

"You won't tell my dad? Or my mom?"

"Don't be silly, Tim. Some problems in retail can't be helped no matter how much effort you put into it."

Timothy ambled away. Foggy watched the boy, shoulders drooped, walk slowly down the center of the path keeping his distance from every display.

He then went to check the front register. Judy, a regular non-magical human resident of Stone Bridge, was already ringing up the first customer of the day, the young Rose.

She spotted Foggy and her face lit up. She reached for one of her items on the counter and held up a brown leather journal with a tattered cover and uneven stitching.

It didn't look familiar, but he figured that it might have just come in.

"This was the only one on the shelf," Rose said. "It's a little banged up. And the pages are mismatched, like a bunch of different books were stuck together. But then I saw that it has this beautiful rose carved into it cover, I mean, how could I not get it? It's like it was meant just for me." She wrapped both her arms around it and clutched it to her bosom. "Did you ever just look at something and think: it's not perfect, but it's so pretty!"

Foggy wondered if the girl realized that her words described herself just as effectively as the book she clasped. He couldn't help but notice that Rose's face beamed, and her aura doubly so. She seemed to him almost like a different person from the meek little girl he'd spoken to a short while ago.

"I'm happy you found what you needed. Be sure to come back soon." And with that, Foggy took off to find an empty shelf where a bunch of used books should've been. "Timothy!" he bellowed once more. *Not that I'm calling his mom*, he thought.

The boy appeared without causing any commotion or destruction. "Yes, Mr. Ramsbottom?"

"Why is this shelf empty? Didn't you stock it this morning? Where are all the grimoires that should be here?"

Timothy swallowed. "In the trash, sir. They were all damaged."

"Damaged?"

"Yes, sir. Like someone had ripped a handful of pages out of each one of them. At first, I thought someone might've done it in anger, but I think it was more of a prank."

"That would be a very destructive and expensive prank. Why do you think that?"

"Because whoever did it, stitched all those missing pages into one book. It had a leather cover with—"

"—A rose carved into it?"

Timothy stared at his boss, unaware that his mouth was hanging open. "How did you know? Did you see it in the break room? I think I left it in there. I can go get it."

He turned to run off, but Foggy reached up and put a heavy hand on his shoulder before the boy could move.

"No. I don't think you can. Don't worry about it, Tim. But do me the favor of making a list of the damaged books. Now if you'll excuse me."

Foggy heard the boy sigh in relief as he walked away to his office. He had an important call to make. Not to the boy's parents, but to the Carrowmore School. It was possible that a cursed grimoire might be heading their way. And it was also possible that the young lady holding it might be much more powerful and much more special than she appeared to be.

It was going to be an interesting semester in Stone Bridge.

Chester's Home for Like-Minded Souls

CHESTER WAS EXCITED FOR TONIGHT. HE KNEW THAT IT WOULD BE THE BEST night of his life, if the anticipation didn't kill him.

Early in the day, he'd arrived at the house with a duffel bag over his shoulder and the key to the front door in his hand. As of this moment, he was a first-time homeowner. In his inside jacket pocket was the paperwork giving him title to the house as long as he could keep up with the mortgage payments. And considering that they practically gave the house away, he'd be paying less now than he had on the monthly rent on his old basement apartment.

Dani, the real estate agent, was reluctant at first to show him the place. Chester assumed it was because he was afraid of scaring off a potential client. However, after reviewing Chester's finances and calculating his most optimistic price range, she just shrugged and figured what the hell.

Their tour of the narrow, two-story house at the end of a quiet lane had been brief, barely long enough to cover the essentials. Chester fell in love with the place, or at least with the idea of owning it from the twisted old oak out front to the backyard overgrown with weeds. He asked Dani if it could be held until he arranged the down payment.

The agent told him that he didn't have to worry. Few prospective buyers lined up for homes that people had died in. Particularly, if some of the deaths were violent and grisly. Also, Chester was told for the sake of full disclosure that it was believed by many that the house was haunted. Neighbors reported that what was likely just a breeze blowing through sounded like moaning. They complained about noises of things that went bump in the night. It was the usual silly stuff, according to Dani, who appeared happy at the thought of closing the file and getting this thing off the market.

Chester wasn't concerned about those rumors. In fact, he had hoped they were true. That was part of the attraction.

The fact that the old house sat at a dead end meant that no one would be stopping in as they passed by on their way to wherever. And Chester was fine with that. After all, his last apartment was just a few houses down from a busy avenue downtown. Yet no one ever happened to pass by. Nobody ever called and said, "Come on down to the café. Join us for a latte," or "We're around the corner having a slice. Wanna meet up?"

It seemed like there wasn't anyone alive who wanted to spend some time with him.

But, he thought, *what about those who weren't alive?*

Most of his first day was spent getting familiar with the place. He didn't own very much so he had little to unpack. The previous owners had left a lot of their furniture, as had the owners before them. There were a few antiques that Chester assumed were even more ancient. Like from the 1950s or earlier, if he had to guess. He'd look it up online once he had the wifi set up. *Maybe*, he thought, *I'll sell a piece or two if I ever need help with the mortgage.*

After exploring the house in the morning, the afternoon was uneventful. By sunset, the only strange thing to happen was that the food delivery man wouldn't come up to the porch. He called Chester and insisted he come out to the curb to get his order.

Chester was a little disappointed and sat in silence as he chowed down on his enchilada. He was almost finished when he thought he heard some things moving around upstairs. It was likely the wind howling through an open window. Maybe it was blowing a creaking door. Or maybe it was something more than that. He smiled and dug into his nachos grande.

At midnight that night, Chester was lying on the old couch. He was watching old anime on his phone when the noises started up again. This time it seemed like they were pulling out all the stops. He could more than just hear the resident spirits rattling, bumping, and dragging. He could also feel their presence in the air around him. The hair on his arms and the back of his neck stood like he was touching an experiment at the Science Center. Chester listened as the wind's whistle transposed down to a lower register until it became more of a moan. Then it transitioned into a series of moans, underscored by near maniacal laughter.

Jumping up, he ran to the plate on the wall and flipped the switch. Light from the Tiffany chandelier shone down on the small country oak dinette. Chester retrieved a checkerboard from his duffel bag, unfolded it, and set it in place. As he put the red and black pieces in place, one checker jumped up from the table. Chester caught it in midair and set it back on its square. When he finished, he stood back and yelled almost loud enough to raise the neighbors, "Anyone want to play a game?"

His voice echoed off the wall but only for a moment before being sucked away, leaving only silence. The house remained absolutely still. It was the quietest since he'd set foot in it that morning. For several minutes, the only sound he heard was his own pulse echoing in his ears. Chester stood there waiting.

Finally, he shook his head and turned away from the table. Chester dragged his feet as he made his way back to the wall plate. He was just about to turn out the light and go to sleep on the couch when he heard the quietest scratching sound. He looked back and saw that a red checker had slid forward.

Smiling, he punched his fist into his palm and shook his hands triumphantly. Two quick steps later, he sat back in the chair next to the board to make his first move. A shrill voice cried out when he put a finger on a black checker. It howled right in his ear when he pushed one onto the next square.

"Whoever that is, if you cut it out right now, you can play the winner." All the crying and howling ceased immediately. Chester smiled and looked at the empty space beyond the other side of the table. "It's your move, friend."

The game continued without any further interruptions.

Chester went on to win six games against multiple opponents. One tried to cheat, but Chester would have none of that funny business. Lucky for him, the other spirits seemed to agree. After losing the seventh match, he acknowledged his invisible opponent with a simple nod, and said, "Good game." Then he yawned and took a seat on the living room couch. "Let me know when it's my turn to play again."

He swiped his phone and started watching another video. But before the opening theme music had finished, he was sound asleep.

When Chester woke the next morning, the sun had already risen. Dawn's first rays were poking through the blinds in the front windows illuminating the dust motes floating lazily in the air. Chester listened a moment and heard checkers still scratching across the board. His grin stretched from ear to ear.

He sat up and grabbed his shoes. He didn't have anything for breakfast, and he needed his coffee. And maybe a bacon, egg & cheese on a roll to go with it. But before he stood up, he looked back at the unattended checker board. He wondered how many others were in the room with him. Enough for a party, maybe? A real kick-ass party?

Now was as good a time as any. Time to go for broke.

"If you guys are interested tonight, besides chess and backgammon, I have all my *D&D* books and dice in my bag." A loud thump caused Chester to jump for the first time since he'd arrived the day before. He turned to see his toppled duffel roll across the floor from the front door all the way to the dinette.

"I'll take that as a 'Yes.'" Chester felt a warmth inside that wasn't coming from the sun shining down on the couch. He was happier than he'd been in a long time. "I think I found my new gaming buddies."

Don't Drink and Divine

THE FIRST FULL MOON OF SPRING WAS THE NIGHT THAT MISTRESS OF THE Night Morena had determined would be best for summoning a familiar. She'd decided on a woodland creature to assist in her spellcasting. That would be the best fit for her branch of magical study. She spent every day since the vernal equinox preparing.

After three months of preparation, that magical March afternoon had finally arrived. Morena opened a special bottle of wine she'd saved to mark the occasion. She enjoyed a glass or two as she took quill in hand to write out the instructions for the ritual. When she finished transcribing, she celebrated with another glass as she reread the scroll, looking for errors. With everything in place, Morena only needed to wait for nightfall. Waiting didn't come easy for her.

When the sun had set beyond the hillside, she packed a bag of necessities. The last item required was wine for the ceremonial cup. Being practical, Morena took a full bottle off the rack instead of the one she'd opened earlier. Half of that one had been drained just to steady her nerves for the night's undertaking. This was more than just inviting a wild animal to share her home. She'd be inviting another living creature to share her being, her spirit.

A little before midnight, Morena grabbed the bag along with her wand and a lantern. She set out into the woods behind her cottage, and walked until she came to a clearing about a mile away. The moon peeked out from behind a cloud, high above the treetops.

A large flat rock presented itself, and Morena set her bag down upon it. Then she began her preparations for casting the summoning spell. She found herself shaking a little. Between her nerves and the chill in the air, she had difficulty just holding the lantern steady. And the flickering, dim light made the scroll difficult to read.

The first step required retrieving a wooden branch of a set length. Morena was delighted to find one with ease nearby. Then, she used it to draw a circle in the dirt by standing in place a slowly spinning about.

Next, she took a pinch of herbs from a pouch, Essence of Nature, which she crushed between her thumb and forefinger over her silver chalice.

"*Alunn balunn dulunn...*" She chanted as the fine dust settled on the bottom of the cup.

"*Regana telava vetaga...*" Setting the chalice down, she took the wine bottle and pulled on the cork. And pulled some more. It was stuck fast. For her third attempt, she placed the bottle between her knees and pulled again. There was a satisfying pop, but she hesitated before pouring. She'd lost her place in the incantation. *Perhaps,* she thought, *I should back up a little.*

"*Regana telava vetaga...*" She poured the wine into the chalice.

Putting the bottle down, Morena shifted the chalice to her right hand. Then she picked up the scroll with her left. No matter how she tilted it she couldn't read the words. The Mistress of the Night set down the chalice and picked up the lantern. *Do I need to have the chalice in my hand?* She read the incantation, put down the lantern and picked up the silver cup again.

"*Leena... melana... dactill... tanono... modris... SPECTIS!*"

Raising the cup in both hands, she placed it to her lips and drank deeply. Then closed her eyes and cleared her mind. She gave no thought to any particular animal. Fox or rabbit, hawk or wren made no difference to her.

When she opened her eyes a minute later, Morena was excited to see what she had summoned. However, as she looked around the clearing, the night was still. No familiar had approached. She thought to grab the lantern but froze. *Will that frighten away any creature lurking in the dark?*

She looked at the ground, then cursed. Morena grabbed the instruction scroll and read it again. *Damn it!* She'd forgotten to pour oil into the circle she'd dug. She would have to repeat the entire process.

A little unsteady from the wine, she bent over to pour the oil into the little trench. She covered every inch, without spilling any within the circle itself. When she'd finished, Morena stood upright and got dizzy. *Too fast, too fast.* The trees didn't spin, but they did seem to move a little. Corking the oil seemed problematic as well.

Taking the cup and the wine, she started the ritual again. "*Regana telava vetaga...*" She poured the wine. "*Leena... melana... dactill... tanono... modris... SPECTIS!*" She drank as greedily as before with her thoughts turning to magnificent beasts that would be as swift as a falcon, or as strong as a bear.

One minute later, she stood alone in the clearing.

"Damn it! The Essence!"

By now, Morena had committed the instructions to memory. She shoved the scroll back into her bag to free both hands. She would track her progress with a checklist in her mind.

Grab the pouch. Take a pinch. Grind the dust. "*Alunn balunn dulunn...*" Pour the wine "*Regana telava vetaga...*" Drink—no, wait, not yet! "*Leena... melana... dactill... tanono... modris... SPECTIS!*" DRINK!

Eyes closed.

Calmness. Serenity.

How long had she have them shut? One minute? Five? When she thought it had been long enough, she slowly raised one eyelid just enough to peek. The full moon was right over the clearing now but no familiar had arrived to answer the call.

Wait, she thought. *What if one had arrived and departed while my eyes were closed?*

"Seven Hells!" she screamed. She pulled the scroll out once more to make sure everything was done in the right order.

Pouch. Pinch. "*AllanBallanDallan!*" Grind. "*Reganatenganavetaga!*" Pour. "*Leena Leena Melena dadill tanno modris SEPTIS!*"

She guzzled the wine, wiped her chin, and held the chalice high in the air so that it shone with the Moon's rays. Morena took a deep breath, closed her eyes, and promptly fell backward. Dropping the chalice, she flailed her arms to break her fall. When she landed, her left hand skid along the ground behind her. It broke the circle and spilled the oil.

"Damn! Damn! Damn!" She crawled along the ground until she found the stick once more, and used it to help her stand.

As she tried to draw another circle, she was unaware of the quiet padding of feet behind her. A stone's throw away, a fox poked its nose from behind the tree line. It quietly watched the scene play out before it.

A voice from above startled the fox. "Hey, did you come to answer the summons?"

The fox saw a falcon sitting on a high branch, also bearing witness to this night's strange event. "No," he replied. "I heard the ruckus from my den, and wondered what was going on. How long has she been at this?"

"*ALABALADALA!!!*" called out the witch in the clearing.

"It's been a while now." The falcon laughed a raspy *kack-kack-kack-kack*. "She doesn't look ready to give in yet."

"No," said another deeper voice emerging from behind them. "She doesn't." The fox and falcon turned and saw a buck with twelve-point antlers, scratching a hoof in the dirt. "It may be a long night for her."

"*TANNOMODROSEPTOS!*"

The three woodland critters watched as the dimly illuminated figure raised her cup aloft once more and then guzzled down its contents.

"Damn it!!" they heard her shout, in frustration as much as anger. "Where are all of you hiding? Why won't you come out?"

Around the edge of the clearing, more and more animals gathered to watch, staying just inside the shadows and outside the lantern light. It would be a long, puzzling, but entertaining night.

No Man Is a Hobbit

THE BATTLE OF 7 AND 3/4 ARMIES RAGED ACROSS THE FIELDS OF Grogenplop. The bastard lord with his bastard sword led a thousand men from the east. The wizened wizard brought his entire order of sorcerers and all of their apprentices to cast spells and rain ice and fire. The warrior priests of Algol came to beat the other cheek while the meek priests of Belgol came to tend the wounded. Elven archers came from inside the Outer Woods of the west, and Dwarves marched out from under the Over Mountains of the north. Motley bands of outlaws and renegades pressed into service fought valiantly even though they all knew the prophecy, "No man may defeat the demon knight."

From dawn to near nightfall, many a knight had fallen slaying the demon hordes with their infernal swords.

As the sun fled to the west, in the middle of the battlefield, two cloaked and hooded figures squared off. One was slight and the other enormous. The larger creature was the fierce demon knight known as Fen the Unclean. He reared up, threw back his cape, and held his axe and mace high. He roared, "For the last time! No! Man! Can! Kill! Me!"

A smirk crossed the lips of his opponent. Arms, seemingly from nowhere and yet everywhere, flung open its cloak to reveal that the warrior was, in fact, three hobbits, each standing on the shoulders of the next. "We are No Men!"

The demonic beast growled. "What infernal deception is this?" He lunged at the three tiny demi-humans, who scattered and formed a triangle about him. A mighty swing of the beast's right arm lowered the axe on the adversary in front of him.

Bibbity Hobbit leapt into the air, avoiding the deadly blade. While still in midair, the diminutive creature drew a full-sized dagger and brought it down through the demon's hand.

The beast howled and dropped his axe. Unable to shake the first hobbit off, Fen took a backhanded swing of his mace toward the second, who waited on his left flank.

Bobbity Hobbit dropped beneath the massive forearm sailing his way and allowed it to pass harmlessly above him. He then reached up and took hold of the massive Unclean hand, and bit down hard. Tears came to the little one's eyes, but neither the bad stench nor the foul taste loosened his jaws.

The demon swung about furiously like a weather vane caught in disputed winds. He thrust both massive, sinewy arms forward, but was unable to shake either demi-human. He tried to clap his hands 'til the hobbits fell off. But they held fast.

In the middle of the frenzy, Fen realized he'd lost track of the last one. *Where did it go?*

The Unclean one no sooner had that thought when he felt the trampling of tiny footsteps running up his back. Little hands grabbed hold of each ear, and a miniature face appeared upside down in front of his own.

"BOO!" it screamed, before planting a long kiss squarely on Fen's grotesquely-shaped, over-sized nose.

With the ferocity of a rock giant hurling boulders at invaders, the demon fighter pounded his massive fists into the ground. Pain shot through his body, but the hobbits hung on. Then the beast threw his head back to loosen the last attacker.

Boo yelled, "bye-ee!" The hobbit jumped free, but not before unsheathing his own dagger. He jabbed it through the beast's cloak and a full inch into its bull-sized back. Boo then rode the dagger to the ground like he was slitting a royal banner, an inglorious feat that he hoped to someday be pardoned for.

"Enough!" the demon yelled. "I cannot be defeated!"

Bibbity and Bobbity drew in close under the demon's defenses. "Can you be de-*kneed*?" they shouted in unison. Then each of them stabbed down on one of the giant's knees from just above the tops of his dragonscale shin greaves.

The mighty Fen the Unclean screamed in a pitch so high only demons could hear it. All of his minions ceased their individual battles to take note of the call. The humans fighting them took advantage of the moment to slice their opponent's individual heads off. The slaughter was swift. Then the fighters began to close around the hobbit three.

Bleeding on the ground, the creature cried out, "I was in the Abyss! How did I end up like this? I was in the Abyss!"

The bastard lord with the bastard sword stepped forward, but the wizened wizard steadied his hand.

"No man," the bearded sage uttered sagely, "may defeat the demon."

"And we're not men!" shouted Bibbity, Bobbity, and Boo.

Then the three Halflings stabbed and sliced the great demon Fen repeatedly. Slice, diced and julienne-fried. Unclean blood spilled out from a thousand cuts, filling furrows and pooling in the parched earth like it was flowing through the loopholes in some ancient prophecy until only an empty husk remained, Fen-free.

All the survivors knelt down in the bloody marsh, except for the older wizards whose back troubles didn't allow them to bow that far. This was followed with many mighty cheers. One man-at-arms proclaimed the three halflings as "the three half-kings." That didn't sit well with the bastard lord but he held his tongue for fear of losing his head.

After that, the hobbits retrieved their cloak and rode off, with Bibbity, Bobbity, and Boo bidding the battle bye-bye.

Maryglen and Her Fairy "Momsters"

ON THE MORNING OF HER TWELFTH BIRTHDAY, MARYGLEN VENTURED INTO the woods to pick apples rather than pick the ripened fruit from the trees in her garden. Then she climbed to the well on the hill to fetch water, rather than use the pump in her own yard. The occasion of her birthday didn't free her from her duties, but she didn't mind. In fact, she enjoyed time away from the house. It was a freedom she was granted only while doing her chores. *A pity*, she thought, *that the "momsters" don't need anything from the market.*

That was the name she had for her two moms, not that she believed for a moment that either of them bore her.

They were fighting again, like two old cats, both territorial and set in their ways. And, as usual, they were arguing about Maryglen and debating their differing plans for her future. Not that the girl who was to live those plans was ever asked for her opinion. She knew that they didn't want that any more than she wanted their future.

Setting down her bucket, Maryglen sat on the hill and looked down into the valley. She selected the best apple from the bunch and bit into it. The *momsters* could fight over the second best like they fought over everything else. For as long as she could remember, she'd been raised by Agatha, the water elemental, and Grizilda, the wood witch. And for just as long, they'd been at each other's throats—sometimes literally. It amazed Maryglen that one mom hadn't killed the other yet and claimed the young maiden as her prize.

Despite her circumstances, she had to laugh. She lived in a humble cottage, but when her fairy not-parents drank too deeply from the casks, they'd spill more than just their wine. They dropped clues about their lives before Maryglen had come along. Agatha had once lived in her own castle in Lake Aweiwego many miles to the east. And Grizilda had grown a mansion of living oak in Werkwood equally as far to the west. However, both fae were forced to live in dreary, agrestic Ruttersdell, midway between their two domains.

And Maryglen was the reason for this great compromise.

To be fair, it was the doings of her actual parents, her birth parents, that caused all this, and it started long before she was born. Many years ago, Agatha saved Maryglen's mother when she surely would've drowned, and in return demanded a "fair" price. Before that, Grizilda had bargained with her father when she rescued him while lost in the forest. Both fairies appeared at the moment of Maryglen's birth. Neither was happy to see the other.

Each petitioned the Unseelie Court. Grizilda argued she had the prior contract. Agatha argued the primacy of the maternal claim to a child. The court ruled that since the parents hadn't known each other when either bargain was struck, nor did they at any time become aware of the other lien, nor had either fae informed the parties involved, they had to share custody of the child until such time as they settled the dispute amongst themselves in whatever matter they saw fit and a final choice was made.

Whatever fate they each had planned for her, Maryglen had never discovered. But so far, those plans had been deferred for a dozen years while the *momsters* tried to bargain, cajole, and trick each other into giving up their claim. They never tried a game of chance that she could remember. *Most likely,* she thought, *because they each feared that the other would be the superior cheater.*

Marglen discarded her apple core. Then she retrieved her bucket and started back down the hill. She could only avoid being home for so long. The fae worried if she was out too long. They weren't afraid she'd run away.

Where could she possibly go?

Their fear was that she might stray too far east or west toward one domain or the other. That would allow one to say that the girl had made a choice. Upon realizing that this was a possibility, Maryglen restricted her own movements, walking the fine line sideways to the sun that kept her away from both places. She wasn't going to make their choice for them.

When she entered the cottage, the two fae put a pin in whatever argument they were having and looked at her instead. Agatha yelled, "Where have you been?"

Maryglen set the apples and water on the table. Then she made a pouty face and cried, "You don't love me!"

The wood witch jumped out of her rocking chair by the fire. "I love you, child! Come to your dear Grizilda!"

"Stay away from her!" Agatha moved to get between the two. She turned to her false daughter and said, "I love you more. It's just that I needed the water to make you a delicious supper. You know I do wonders with water, my dear. Oh, you'll love it."

Grizilda shoved the other aside. "And I needed the apples for the scrumptious pie I was going to bake for you."

With a final sniffle, Maryglen's fake tears dried up. "Okay. Thank you, mother. And thank you, too, mother. I love both of you, too. I'll go wait in my room for supper then."

When the door closed behind her, she heard the fighting start again. She climbed onto the bed the wood witch had crafted for her, and crawled under the expensive hand-stitched quilt the water elemental had purchased for her to top it. Neither *momster* had mentioned her birthday, and Maryglen chose not to remind them. Better to let them forget the day and forget her age.

Four more years, Maryglen thought. The court had ruled that they had shared custody of the *child*. But she'd read all the books in the library and discovered something important. She knew that after her sixteenth birthday, she was no longer a child under fae law, and neither could claim custody any longer. She could petition the Unseelie Court herself. They may be reluctant to hear the pleas of a human living among them, but they'd been unsympathetic to the *momsters* before.

Failing that, she'd try the Seelie Court. Maybe they would claim her since she didn't have a twisted bone in her body like a gnarly wood witch, or wretched blood coursing through her like a water elemental.

And after she'd won her freedom, she would find a way back to her own world. Once there, she would try to find her real parents. All she knew of them were their names: Mary and Glen. But she would do whatever she had to do and find them any way she could. As long as she didn't have to sell her own firstborn to do it.

Thrice-Told Tavern Tales, Retold

Two roads diverged in a wood, and I—I couldn't tell you which one I took. Not that remembering would make all that much of a difference. Truth be told, the road has diverged at least five times already. I didn't always take the left, but I'm not sure which one was a right. But before I had to make another choice, I decided to turn south, off the beaten path. At least, I think it was south. Those roads were twisty, and I couldn't see the sun above the canopy.

This is usual for me. I tend to get lost a lot. Maps? I have trouble reading and following them. And I've lost or broken a dozen compasses that friendly folks have gifted me to set me straight. But Mother Nature has her own way of speaking to me. Or maybe the rustling of leaves you hear is secretly a bunch of wood nymphs whispering on the wind.

Whatever the reason, my sense of misdirection tends to yield positive results. Just when I thought I should turn back, as if I knew which way to turn back to, I heard the babble of water just beyond a clump of trees. And yet it didn't seem like any brook I'd known before.

And that's when I came upon the legendary Boiling River of Agvobar. Instead of a steady current, the river had a turbulent flow from circular swirling eddies that bubbled up to the surface. The bubbles burst releasing wave upon wave of steam. I dropped my bag so I could find my camera and record the images. However, by the time I was ready to film, the maelstrom had settled back into a regular river. Quite tame.

I stepped forward cautiously, and a wave lapped the shore, spraying me. I covered my face, only to realize that cool water had struck me. The boiling had ceased. Cautiously, I stepped into the water and felt the current on my legs. As I walked out, I came upon gold coins and other artifacts dropped by others who'd tried to cross before me. While I was gathering up some of the coins, I felt the ground shift slightly beneath me. A chill went up my spine that had nothing to do with the water.

Fleeing as fast as I could, I made my way back to the bank and hauled myself onto land just as the rumbling started. There was a flash of steam and the bubbling water boiled again. Frightened as I was by my narrow escape, I gathered my belongings and fled back into the wood. I told my friends at my campsite of my discovery. They didn't believe me. Then I showed them the one 18th century doubloon I'd manage to salvage; I watched them drool at the image of Charles I. They demanded that I show them where I'd found it, so I agreed to take them there. The promise of more gold coins, centuries old, was too much of a lure for them to turn down.

Unfortunately, I got us all lost trying to find the river again.

"What do you mean I have to get a job? I'm dead! This is heaven!" Todd sputtered, surprised that he even had breath or spittle. "It's the afterlife. Eternal rest granted and all that."

The ethereal form before him shook his head slowly from side to side and opened the book in his hand.

"Do not allow the lack of brimstone and flames and suffering deceive you. You have not yet reached Heaven. This..." He spread him arms and turned his head to indicate the vast, empty grayness about them. *"This is Purgatory."*

Todd turned and searched the distance. There was nothing to be seen. No angels. No harps. No Pearly Gates. Just a gray desert wasteland. It was like he'd been placed in his own personal limbo.

"Purgatory? But that's sort of good, right? I'm on my way to Heaven, right? How long do I have to stay here?"

The figure turned the book about so Todd could read it. It was a ledger.

"Until you have paid for your sins. Which brings us back to your job placement. Are you good with your hands? There are many nursing homes which need skilled laborers to answer some prayers."

For all the times Todd had heard his name cursed, he could only imagine it being used in prayer. He leaned forward, taking hold of the book and scanning its pages. "You got any orphanages needing people? I think I work better with kids than old people. I had... issues with my dad."

"Yes," the form stated. *"That is part of why you're here. You'll get out of here quicker if you face your transgressions and assist the elderly."*

Todd returned the book to the desk. "So what I'm hearing you say is that I can still get out of here and into Heaven by assisting little kids."

The ethereal form shut the book and sat quietly for a minute. *"Sure."*

My guests milled about the parlor swaying with the music from the antique victrola, chatting away mindlessly. Each held a drink casually in one hand while gesturing more animatedly with the other. The food platters had gone untouched so far.

Standing by the bay window, I looked out at the full moon, shining down upon the house on this cloudless night. Then I lowered my eyes and stared down the drive and the empty road beyond it.

I planned this party so long ago. Months of my life were spent in preparation for this night. Waiting for midnight to arrive to welcome the first chapter in my new life.

As the clock rang out a quarter to the hour, an unsurprisingly strong hand settled on my shoulder. I turned to see a short, raven-haired woman in a red dress. I hadn't seen Councilwoman Madeline in years, but this was exactly how I remembered her.

"Are you enjoying the evening?" I asked.

"It's okay," she said in a flat monotone voice. "But when do I get to kill my double?"

I sighed.

Tonight was to be my night for revenge on all who had ever wronged me. I'd installed trap doors to oubliettes and pits filled with impaling spikes. The adjoining room was set to fill with gas. The walls in the hall beyond were set to slowly close and crush the occupants. Alcoves had been readied in the basement to imprison bodies, dead or alive, behind walls of brick and mortar. The carefully crafted cuisine was laced with rat poison and the punch bowl spiked with arsenic. I could even promise the guests some amontillado … but it would be a promise unkept.

Looking around the room, I spied business associates, rivals, a former boss, even a mentor who thought I'd never amount to anything. Individuals who had wronged me and wounded me grievously. They'd caused to me to lose great fortunes and status. Inside my parlor, I gazed upon the faces of these people whom I invited to my house of death so I could hear their screams and see them die.

However, every one of these who stood and swayed and danced and laughed before me was a fake. Each was an imitation that I created to sincerely flatter not them but myself. Each robotic double I'd painstakingly constructed was but an image of one of this evening's victims. They were marvelous. Brilliant.

And yet my heart fell heavy as I watched my masterpieces converse and interact. They behaved and socialized like ordinary people. Yet every one of these doppelgangers was ready to kill and replace their human counterparts. My dear Madeline, with steel for bones, was strong enough to stuff her duplicate halfway up the chimney.

I'd planned that they would go out into the world and wreak havoc in all the lives they encountered. Once that task was completed, they would disappear, shedding their identities, and leaving only tragic, bitter memories in their wake.

I looked back into faux-Madeline's sparkling but lifeless blue eyes in a way I'd never dare do with the original. In a way that I'd never care to do. I placed my hand alongside her face, touched her soft pale skin.

"You won't get to, I'm afraid. She hasn't come. No one came. I can only surmise that they all hate me as much as I despise them."

She pouted. That made me smile. I ran my thumb along her cheek down to her lips. Then I slid my hand beneath her chin. Leaning down, I pressed my lips to hers. A kiss to close the book on my old life. She had no reaction to it at all, just a blank stare.

The moment passed. I realized that I had no feeling for my creations. And they had none for me. But with the absence of any animosity, I couldn't visit my wrath upon them. Sealing androids into the basement walls would do nothing to satisfy my revenge. I stood defeated.

"Then what shall we do now?" she asked.

I clinked my glass to hers. "Cheers," I said, as I raised my glass and drank.

It was a pleasant first date with Susan. I had the primavera; she, the penne a la vodka. The bottle of the house red complemented both meals. The conversation, though, was a bit awkward. We tried to steer away from work, without getting bogged down in oversharing too much personal information.

Behind Susan, I could see the two men in suits sitting at the bar. Each had a tall seltzer in front of him. The guy on the left had a Lemon wedge, on the right Lime. Those are the names I associated with them. Every now and then, I'd spy Lemon looking back at me, or Lime glancing over toward Susan. When they weren't looking at me directly, they were keeping eyes on me through the mirror.

This continued through most of the meal, but I managed to maintain my focus on Susan. When the waitress brought me a drink, she placed a napkin in front of me. On it was a note that simply said "RUN". I folded it over once and stuffed it into my pocket.

That piqued Susan's curiosity. "What was that, Mr. Vice President?"

"Oh, just a note from a fan with a suggestion for the future."

Susan's eyes twinkled as she sipped her wine. "I may have a suggestion for the future, sir. Though I fear I can't see anything beyond tomorrow's breakfast."

I raised my left hand and flashed a signal to the men at the bar. Lemon started for the door, and Lime came to the table.

"Susan, I'm terribly sorry," I said as I started to stand. "But something has come up that requires my attention. Renford here will see you home."

She put her wine glass down and was about to rise. "Mr. Stone, that won't be nec—"

My hand was raised. "Please, I insist. Enjoy your dinner. The chicken is wonderful, and the *crème brulee*, I hear, is to die for."

I left without another word. It was disappointing to miss out on a delightful evening. After that might've been a night to remember, but I fear I wouldn't be around to enjoy the French toast in the morning. I wasn't ready to die for a dessert or a night of passion.

Sadly, the note hadn't been from a fan. And the next time I saw Susan would be through a two-way mirror. At least, I left her with a better last meal than I would've had.

Sitting on his ornate throne, the king looked down at the bound prisoner kneeling before him. "Clementus, the charges against you are grave, and the evidence is strong. Do you have any words before I pass judgment?"

"I request trial by combat," he coughed out between breaths. "And I pray my champion has arrived."

The king nodded. "That is your right." He looked up and addressed the assembled crowd. "Who will serve as his second and fight the royal champion on his behalf?"

A curtain of silence fell over the court, torn asunder when a commanding voice boomed, "I shall!" The crowd parted as a seven-foot-tall warrior emerged. He carried a sword in each hand and marched on four legs. The bare-chested creature was adorned with a braided, gold torc about his throat and stag antlers upon his brow.

Spectators gasped at the sight. None could deny it. It was Garrukkus, God of the Hunt, in the flesh. Many fell prostrate before his massive form. Others shielded their eyes from the brilliance of his aura. Some stood transfixed and basked in his majesty. All to the displeasure of the king.

Garrukkus strode up to the prisoner, sheathed his swords, and addressed the court. "Clementus, a loyal, faithful servant, beseeched for deliverance. I am here to answer his prayer." He folded his two massive hands together and raised them above his head. "I shall fight on his behalf!"

The king, unimpressed, waved a hand to his speaker. "Call my Champion."

The speaker declared, "The King's Champion will come forward!"

There were murmurs in the crowd as people were jostled aside. The God of the Hunt waited, more in boredom than anticipation, as a soldier stepped from the masses holding a spear at the ready.

The God of the Hunt reared up and laughed at the man. "You would try to kill me with that. You think you can kill a god with a spear?"

The stone-faced soldier waited for the laughter to die. "My name is Longinus. And you wouldn't be the first god this spear has killed."

A shadow emerged from the front door, followed quickly by the human who cast it. In two steps, he was at the edge of the porch. In the next, he leapt down the stairs.

"Roger! Please, wait!" A frightened but serene voice called out into the night. It belonged to a beautiful young woman who appeared in the doorway. The word "statuesque" didn't do justice to one sculpted like a Greek goddess. When the sound of her voice reached Roger's ears, he halted and turned to face her. He turned around to face her. Then he stood perfectly still, entranced. Only his eyes moved, bearing witness to each graceful step as she descended the front stoop. For two months, Clio had been his world, and he'd been attracted to her as sure as gravity held him to the ground.

"Clio, I promised you, I'll keep your secret. But I have to go." He struggled to move. "Please, let me go."

"Sweetheart." Her voice was a soft whisper on the wind. "I told you that you might be a little shocked to meet Mom and Dad. Please, come back inside."

Roger felt the tug inside him, pulling on him to return to the house. He shrugged it off when he saw Clio's parents step out onto the porch. Her mother, standing a little over six feet tall, was a brown and white furry, fluffy rodent who looked like she could tuck Roger into a pouch in her cheeks. Her father, under five feet, had the hairy legs of a goat and the ears to match. He was a naked human from the waist up, clutching a set of pipes, the musical kind, in one hand, and a golden goblet in the other.

"I know you warned me, Clio, but this is more — so much, much more — than I expected." And with that, the human broke free of her attraction and fled. He'd thought he'd found the love of his life. But her mother was a hamster and her father smelt of elderberries.

The party wanted nothing more than to escape, but they got turned around in the maze of underground corridors. Their search for stairs leading out of the catacombs ended when they stumbled into a torch-lit chamber that was filled with more than just the dearly departed. The room was lousy with skeletal remains. And in the center stood a robed and hooded figure.

"It's the necromancer," Theodora whispered with her last bit of breath. It echoed off the chamber's walls.

"No." The figure raised an arm in protest. "I am… not… a necromancer!" He pushed back his hood to reveal a face of tight, dried gray skin with sunken eyes. His garish red lips were pulled back away from his dazzling white teeth with diamond inserts. Flickering torches caused shadows to dance across his features.

"Then… what are you?" asked Frawley, the group leader.

"I… am…"

With a flourish and a speed unexpected in the aged figure, he whipped off the cloak and twirled it about over his head. Beneath, he was dressed in a white suit, studded with sequins that caught and reflected every glimmer of light in the chamber. "…a necro*dancer*!"

He clapped his hands together twice. All the skeletons rattled their bones and jumped to attention. The party, as a whole, took a step backward, unprepared for the battle that was to come. With another clap from their master, the skeletons swarmed together. Not into a battle line, but into a conga line.

A loud *Crack!* rang in everyone's ears. Then the room was filled with the popping of phalanges, the clapping of metacarpals, and the tapping of metatarsals, as twenty-four-hundred-and-ninety-six bones, eschewing sinew, and abandoning tendon, moved freely and furiously in tandem like the framework of one great, well-oiled machine.

Raised arms shook and rattled like maracas and mandibles chattered like castanets. When they reached the musical bridge, the mage threw two dozen wands into the air. Each skeleton caught a pair and then coupled with the dancer next to them. Facing each other, they played their partners' rib cages with absolute precision.

In their final phase of their last movement, the squad of twelve turned their attention toward their captive audience. They arrayed in a line, ready for battle. They hurled their batons up and away, before locking arms in a near-impenetrable wall. Then they closed in on the party, with a *Step! Kick! Step! Kick!* before falling to their patellas with a clattering crescendo!

"Because," called out the mage, flailing his arms beside him. "It ain't no sin to take off your skin and dance around in your bones!"

Frawley was the first to recover. He was slow to find his voice. "We'd rather keep our skin where it is."

"For now, you may," their host said. "But this is still a Dance-Off, so line up now or admit your defeat!"

On a hot, dry afternoon long ago, I left my farm and went to see a big city. It was a more magical place than I could've imagined. It was teeming with people, each of whom was a story worthy of telling, and so many stories were I told. However, I didn't stay there long. I chose instead to travel to bigger cities over the mountains and across the seas.

I saw the pinnacles of civilizations and their pits of despair. Empires grew in size before me, even as they shrank into the dust in my wake. I tarried long enough to feel power surge within me, but always soldiered forward before any inevitable corruption could take hold.

The journey rejuvenated my old heart and sore muscles. I ventured so far that I may have circled the known world until one day, after many years, I returned to the fields in which I used to toil. Many times before then I'd stopped and told my stories of the places I'd gone, the wonders I'd seen, and the people I'd met. And the magic I felt. I'd recounted them time and again to some nameless farmers, sometimes in exchange for a drink of water. And maybe for a few moments, they wouldn't feel like nobody, but like someone who could be somebody.

Maybe one day, one of them will pass my field and tell me a tale of the magic and wonder they'd witnessed.

About the Author

Christopher J. Burke is a writer, high school math teacher, and webcomic creator. He's also a gamer and fan of science fiction who has been telling stories since he was little. This combination ultimately led to his first professional sale, "Don't Kill the Messenger," in *Autoduel Quarterly* in 1988. This was followed by the creation of a fiction fanzine, *Driving Tigers Magazine*, with stories set in the Car Wars universe of Steve Jackson Games, which had a five-issue run. Thanks to his knowledge and love of that game, he was asked to co-author *GURPS Autoduel*, 2nd edition for Steve Jackson Games.

He took time off from writing when he switched careers and went back to school to become a teacher. But not before he completed a goal of having a humor piece published in *MAD Magazine*. In 2007, he started the math-based webcomic *(x, why?)*, filled with the kind of geeky humor that makes his students groan when he includes them in the daily lesson. Christopher still updates the comic with new strips every week on his blog. http://mrburkemath.blogspot.com.

After a chance meeting at a launch party in 2014, Christopher was once again bitten by the writing bug and started producing flash fiction. He won several monthly flash fiction contests on the eSpec Books blog, which then published a collection of his short fiction, *In A Flash 2020*.

His most recent stories, "Portrait of a Lady Vampire" and "Bringer of Doom", appeared in *Daily Science Fiction* and in the anthology *Devilish & Divine*, from eSpec Books. His work has appeared in online magazines such as *MetaStellar*, *Free Flash Fiction* and *Short Beasts*. In 2023, he launched the first in a series of mini-books with the title Burke's Lore Briefs.

Christopher lives in Brooklyn with his wife, Antoinette.

Our Magical Moonbeams

Abigail Reilly
Alex Jay Berman
Andrew Kaplan
Andy Holman Hunter
Anthony R. Cardno
Aysha Rehm
Bailey A Buchanan
Barry Nove
Benjamin Adler
bill
Bill & Kelley & Kyle
Brendan Coffey
Brian D Lambert
Brian Klueter
Brooks Moses
Buddy Deal
Caitlin Rozakis
Candi O'Rourke
Carla Spence
Carol J. Guess
Carol Jones
Caroline Westra
Cheri Kannarr
Christine Lawrence
Christine Norris
Christopher Bennett
Christopher J. Burke
Coats Family
Colleen Feeney
Craig "Stevo" Stephenson
Crysella
Dale A Russell

Danielle Ackley-McPhail
Danny Chamberlin
Denise and Raphael Sutton
Doniki Boderick-Luckey
Donna Hogg
Duane Warnecke
E.M. Middel
Ef Deal
Ellen Montgomery
Emily Weed Baisch
Erin A.
"filkertom" Tom Smith
Frank Michaels
Gary Phillips
Gav I
GhostCat
GraceAnne Andreassi
    DeCandido
Greg Levick
Ian Harvey
J.E. Taylor
Jack Deal
Jakub Narębski
James Aquilone
Jamie René Peddicord
Jennifer Hindle
Jennifer L. Pierce
Jeremy Bottroff
Joe Gillis
John Keegan
John L. French
John Markley

Jonathan Haar
Judy McClain
Karen Palmer
KC Grifant
Kelly Pierce
Ken Seed
kirbsmilieu
krinsky
Lark Cunningham
LCW Allingham
Lee
Lee Thalblum
Lisa Kruse
Liz DeJesus and Amber Davis
Lorraine J Anderson
Louise Lowenspets
Lynn P.
Maria V Arnold
Marie Devey
Matthew Barr
Michael A. Burstein
Michael Barbour
Morgan Hazelwood
Mustela
Niki Curtis
Paul Ryan
pjk
Rachel A Brune
Raja Thiagarajan
Reckless Pantalones
Rich Gonzalez
Rich Walker

Richard Fine
Richard Novak
Richard O'Shea
Rigel Ailur
Robert Greenberger
Robert Ziegler
Ronald H. Miller
Ruth Ann Orlansky
Scott Schaper
Shawnee M
Shervyn
Sheryl R. Hayes
Sonia Koval
Sonya M.
Steph Parker
Stephen Ballentine
Stephen W. Buchanan
Steven Purcell
Subrata Sircar
Susan Simko
The Creative Fund by BackerKit
Thomas Bull
Thomas P. Tiernan
Tim Tucker
Tom B.
Tracy Popey
Tracy 'Rayhne' Fretwell
Will "scifantasy" Frank
'Will It Work' Dansicker
William C Tracy
wmaddie700